The Time Being

The Time Being

Mary Meigs

For Sal and Véro —
and the wonderful
English connection —
from Mary Meigs

Talonbooks

1997

Published with the assistance of the Canada Council.

Talonbooks
#104—3100 Production Way
Burnaby, British Columbia
Canada V5A 4R4

Typeset in Garamond and printed and bound in Canada by Hignell
Printing Ltd.

First Printing: October 1997

Talonbooks are distributed in Canada by General Distribution Services, 30
Lesmill Road, Don Mills, Ontario, Canada M3B 2T6; Tel.: (416) 445-3333;
Fax: (416) 445-5967.

Talonbooks are distributed in the U. S. A. by General Distribution Services
Inc., 85 Rock River Drive, Suite 202, Buffalo, New York, U.S.A. 14207-2170;
Tel.: 1-800-805-1083; Fax: 1-800-481-6207.

Canadian Cataloguing in Publication Data

Meigs, Mary, 1917-
  The time being

  ISBN 0-88922-374-2

  I. Title.
PS8576.E39T56 1997   C813'.54   C97-910853
PR9199.3.M44T56 1997

With thanks as ever to Carole Robertson with her awesome computer skills and genius for deciphering rough copies, and to Lise Weil and Mary Schendlinger, my indispensable readers and counsellors. And thanks for encouragement along the way from Marie-Claire Blais, Jane Rule, Helen Sonthoff, Judy Adamson, Yvonne Klein and Marisa Zavalloni.

And to my editors, Karl and Christy Siegler, who have made me feel welcome at Talon Books.

To my faraway friend in Australia.

Chapter One

The real story is truer than fiction, Marj once thought. And the story that is born in the imagination, the vision of phantom bodies growing close to one another, precisely touching with imagined hands that rove knowingly, and the awful daring of imagined mouths joining lightly, then with a passion that sends tremors coursing down the two bodies, so many miles apart? They—two old women—are separated by a continent, by the Pacific Ocean and the International Date Line, that imaginary line in obedience to which real people turn their watches forward or backward and re-tune their bodies, temporarily upside down. If one of them outraces the sun, the next day is the day she left. Somewhere, in Australia or in Canada, that day has been lived or is going to be lived. "It's your yesterday," the woman in Australia will say on the telephone, and the woman in Canada will answer, "It's your tomorrow."

Their story begins with a letter from Kate to Marj, a blue airletter full of Australian sunshine, with Ayer's Rock burning red in the desert in the upper left-hand corner. The name and address (how she got hold of the address will become the preamble to Kate's saga of their meeting) in blue ink runs lightly along, leans forward, holds back, in the six printed letters of CANADA. Marj, who dabbles in graphology, stares at the blue letter and sees a woman whose exuberance is tempered by a lifetime of discipline. The contents of the letter have sent Marj's spirits soaring in the June air. It is from an invisible woman, both impersonal and warmly personal. She writes about Marj's work with the authority of someone used to analyzing and judging books; she writes a fan letter, keeping herself out of it, but immediately alive in Marj's mind. Kate has thought hard about the words of her letter and how they must contain the right amount of praise, not fulsome but studied; she writes from her experience as a teacher responsible for the opening of minds; she has handled the dynamite of judgement with practised care. She is delighted to be able to praise; she has felt a kindred spirit in Marj's autobiography. She has seen Marj in a semi-documentary film about seven old women, a globe-trotting film. She has liked the slow-speaking woman in the film. She waits with a certain impatience, slipping into a sense of being rebuffed as the weeks and months roll by with no answer from Canada. Seven months. She cons herself into thinking: so she doesn't answer; that's cool. And suppresses the voice saying, she's thinking: just another fan letter—I won't answer right away. And bursts in to a crescendo: who does she think she is? She sees the slightly bent, tall body of Marj, hears her diffident speech, drawling a bit. After the seventh month has gone by, Kate consigns Marj to a dark corner of her mind where Marj's silence lives as a small rejection. Eventually, in Australia, she will exhume the buried question, the why of those seven months and Marj will wriggle like a worm on a fish hook.

Summer slips into autumn and into the winter of a new year. Kate's letter has sifted downward in a pile of unanswered mail and Marj discovers it, rereads it, feels guilty, answers, sends her new book. The real story, the love between two old women, can begin now with a rush, powered by the seven-month wait.

Their letters—pre-meeting—love's embryo warm and nourished in amniotic fluid where it grows without hindrance. Each of the women, one in her late sixties, the other in her middle seventies, thrives in this medium of letters and is rejuvenated. Each in her separate life listens to music and breaks into spontaneous dance; in one of her correct premonitions, Marj sees Kate put on a tape and dance to it. Kate, with her mind's eye, sees the lively but disjointed efforts of Marj and smiles indulgently. Visions are released by the letters, as close to the truth (the truth of love, all-noticing, all-remembering) as human beings can get, with no ill-effects or hangovers. As Marj rereads the letters, she is struck by the perfection of their falling-in-love, the high-soaring duet they sing, in which their old voices sound young and each tries to outdo the other by demonstrating her purity of heart, each in an innocent rivalry which holds difference in suspension, biding its time. Kate is the first to notice the cloud just below the surface, recognizes a familiar trouble, differing views about the demands of love. To Kate, love demands readiness to sacrifice in its name: self, the very thing that Marj has cultivated, letting love take second place. It is her creative self, closely guarded; Kate knows this from Marj's books, in which the writer falls in love and temporarily yields up her soul, only to snatch it back. And here is Marj writing, six months before they meet, "Being 'in love' with you means that I yield up to you without regret my solitary autonomy, that we hold each other in trust and literally..." It probably occurs to Kate that this is a load of codswallop (her Australian word for nonsense) and that Marj isn't going to yield up a thing. But she wants to believe and she loves Marj's naïve eloquence; she herself dreams of a marriage of true minds in which each yields and blends into a single consenting mind, greater than the sum of its parts, and a single consenting body. She puts on her tape of *Cabaret* and belts out her signature song. "Maybe this time I'll be lucky," she sings. "Maybe this time he'll stay," and holds out her arms in yearning. Hasn't she herself yielded up her decision never to fall in love again? Hasn't she put aside her knowledge that, after ten years, she is still spooked by the loss of her younger lover, is suspicious of love and its inevitable disappointments? But she lets joy possess her and rides the crest of the big wave which rolls in so triumphantly, and tries not to think of the flotsam almost hidden in Marj's hyperbole.

Loud! Loud! Loud!
Loud I call to you, my love!

The pace of their letters quickens until each is writing the other every day. At first they waited for answers; now the letters crisscross in the vast space, the half a world between them. Identical thoughts cross; they quote the same poets, they love the same composers, they have read the same books. Now they are dwelling in the Shangri-La of their much younger selves when they greedily soaked up the father-culture and were possessed by the voices of its great love-poets. In no time at all, it seems, they are talking about their love. "Have I gone over the top, I wonder?" writes Kate, and Marj answers, "There is no top." It only takes Kate's photograph and her first telephone call, her musical voice and purring laugh, to release a dammed-up flood in each of them, rolling over time and space. "You draw out of me green leaves and flowers," says Marj. They speak with the tongues of women and angels, their new speech, and with the old vocabulary of love. "It seems to be coming from somewhere deep inside, some dark warm cavern from which no sound has issued for a very long time," says Kate. She trembles when she sees a letter from Marj in the mailbox; is that a sign that she is in love? Kate addresses the question, am I in love? (for Marj has come out with it—

12

"I've fallen in love with you," on the telephone) just as she addresses every important and difficult question; she seeks evidence and logical explanation. She trembles. Is it love to tremble? She tries to hang on to the rational, sceptical part of her mind. She reminds herself and Marj that they are "two elderly women" (perhaps a subject of ridicule?) and braces herself against the torrent of Marj's response. "'Two elderly women' in whom reside the great lovers in their prime," Marj answers. Marj loves the sound of her own voice, thinks Kate; she has read Marj's books and knows her unreliability. She throws herself into love and slithers out of it. Take it easy, says Kate to herself, reaching out for a handhold. "I've been telling myself for years that I'm not capable of something *quite* as exciting and zestful as *falling* in love...and I'm sticking to this safe belief! That I'm past it! But I'm certainly *capable* of LOVE."

Kate loves the woman who has had the "huge courage" to come out publicly as a lesbian, she says, and she loves Marj's "scary honesty about the oppressive obsession that is (or isn't?) love." Honesty. Marj thinks about it; in her books, she tells Kate, there is always "a precious remnant of dishonesty." To herself she says that the precious remnant is what the writer leaves out that would tip the scales; the measure of it is the measure of her cowardice. "What one feels it's safe to be honest about," she explains to Kate. "The dishonesty lies in what I'm ashamed of, that might compromise the reader's liking for me." Each believes that nothing can compromise their liking for each other. "I've been thinking about security," says Marj, "feeling secure in your care, what that means. It means everything. It's the deep meaning of love.... It's our arms around each other even when they're not." She compares their love to Beethoven's Waldstein sonata; her interrogation begins. "Who are you? Tell me!" "She wants to know who I am!" writes Kate. "I held back; don't rush it...and posted my 'confessions'.... So...in Waldsteinian fashion, the 'extraordinary stillness' and the beautiful 'almost timidly stated' phrase are gone, and the eager, impetuous 'more and more' have taken off!! and I have introduced myself to you…and wondered and feared…until your response, and I am safe! '*Our* kind of friendship is something I welcome with a tender welcome,' you say…. You seem to trust me, to let me into your mind (and heart)…the stuff of our kind of friendship." Marj writes, "I love you with no fear of your anger, for your ability to defuse any possibility of anger."

"…I yield up to you without regret my solitary autonomy…we hold each other in trust and literally." "That says it all," Kate writes. Marj, four months after her first letter to Kate, has soared over the top that has no top and believes every word she says. She is sure that she has never in her life felt so joyfully incautious. "This morning, May 21," Kate writes, "she has said she'd put her arms around me and kiss me on the MOUTH. There's a wicked little part of me that wants to chuckle at our mutual 'properness,' our mutual avoidance of the three-letter word…. But we're already there," she says and quotes Marj again: "Profound tenderness," "a sharing of all our identities," "tes mains dans mes mains." "There'll be a wonderful physical *closeness*," says Kate. "We're not going to disappoint each other, because by the time we meet (if not already) we'll *know* each other and have appropriate expectations. I'm not in need of 'Wild Nights'"—[she quotes Emily Dickinson]—for Marj has been suddenly cautious in her letters: "no tearing of our pleasure with rough strife," she counsels. "Age will save me from desire in its usual sense," she speaks of her "love-angsts." So Kate sends tender reassurance and with it, the certainty for Marj of the warmth of Kate's knowledgeable body. "We speak the same language of love in *all* its manifestations," Kate says. "We've sort-of made love already…and orgasms are not compulsory." Reading this, Marj laughs out loud.

14

"Tu es bien dans ta peau," Marj writes. She has read signs in Kate's relaxed handwriting which fills each page from edge to edge, and in her voice, mezzo-soprano, tenderly sensual yet unalarming to Marj who is easily alarmed. Her reading of signs tells her that Kate has been at home in her body since the day she was born and that she knows, as well, the power of her radiant eyes. She has never felt the misery of a body that doesn't know what to do with itself. "We were a touchy family," Kate will tell Marj. "Touchy-feely." Their parents did not instill in their children a sense of bodily shame; rather, a sense of ease, unlike Marj's parents, who were not bien dans leur peaux and thought it improper for anyone else to be. Now Marj yields to Kate, body and soul, she says: "I of little faith am full of faith *in us*. I embrace you with prolonged tenderness, this all in the passionate fullness of time." Marj is "a passionate Puritan," says Kate. They begin to describe their bodies. Kate says that she is "over-endowed in the boob department"; she adds that this "may reduce the arousal quotient." She says that Marj has a "boyish" body. Marj answers that *her* body is "under-endowed in most departments. Some would call me flat-chested." She says that Kate seems to have an inexhaustible power to arouse.

From the beginning Marj has read Kate, first from every-thing she hasn't said, then from what she says—in words and in the excitable energy of her handwriting, rich with exclamation points, underlining, multiple question marks—the nearest thing to speech. "You are younger than I am but not fatally younger," she writes after Kate's first telephone call. "Your father was (conceivably is) a minister. [A long shot] Clearly I'm much more selfish than you are." For Kate has confessed to having a Pollyanna in herself, the compulsion to help people, which she'd inherited from her mother. "I've been working at killing her off, giving her less power." "The quality of your kindness unstrained (mine is strained to the breaking point sometimes)," replies Marj. "People come to you to be warmed," she says. "And it's not a quid pro quo." She says that Kate's kindness is partly inherited, perhaps; she has read that every bird makes its own version of the basic song, depending on its talent as a singer. Kate meanwhile has told Marj that she isn't selfish: "you have a very healthy respect for yourself," she says.

"Our worst selves are in love," Kate writes. Marj has forgotten that her worst self is the one who can't love. They have made guileless confessions to each other: Kate says that she has been told that she has charisma; Marj says that she likes to be made much of. "We recognize each other's worst selves," she says, "(or what each swears is her worst self) *as our own*—with a kind of forgiving delight. But you must tell me sometime what you think yours is, since I only know you have one when you tell me so." She invents a story, according to which the priest at Kate's baptism cries out, "But this child has no original sin!"

The time of beatitude, of perfect equilibrium, when each is in the other's mind and skin, when each feels unquestioning reverence for the other. "You read me and feel me," says Marj, "and you respond to my letters without misunderstanding a single word. I love the reality of loving you—truly being tuned by your perfect love-pitch." She proposes that they write a book together: "*our* time being, our happening…a kind of continental counterpoint. Each of us would keep her voice." "Our book *The Time Being*," Kate answers. "I like the juxtaposition of tenderness and passion and time in relation to US, that TIME has actually permitted (for me) and has (it would seem) actually *insisted* that we meet!" Their book will set the seal on their trust, each in each. Marj has screened out every intimation of trouble, sharp rocks just under the shining surface. She will come to her senses later, in Australia, when Kate will be gently vague, when in due course their book together will divide into two books, each a monument to their love, and to the discovery of their differences.

The hubris of love. Marj has a severe case of it. She feels invincible. Now and then, to be sure, her ear has been struck by a bass note, the note of fear, that sounds at intervals in Kate's letters while the melody races and tumbles above it. Sometimes that one note grows in volume to a crescendo of unbearable intensity silently sounding in Marj's head. It intrudes on the space of trust, their safe haven in which agreement is assumed. In the course of their long telephone calls before they meet, Kate may suddenly fall silent with a silence as vast as the space between them, and Marj recognizes it as the mute and stubborn speech of disagreement. She has said something that triggers fear in Kate and danger for herself. Their words have stopped running impulsively toward each other, joyfully innocent words, Marj has supposed, without any power to hurt. It is her first lesson in Kate's vulnerability, how it can scramble a sentence she hears and make it lethal for herself. Agreement has been assumed, for two women who love each other think that because of all their proven identities, each can know the other's thoughts. "Our duet for two voices in unison," writes Marj from her state of hubris. She dares to tell Kate what she is thinking and why she is thinking it. She knows from experience but chooses to ignore it, that she is treading in one of ego's sacred groves. Now, however, on the telephone she has the sense to be afraid. The next evening (Kate's morning) she calls Kate, and Kate's voice enters directly into Marj's left ear; it vibrates and Marj sees a bow drawn lightly over the strings of a superb old violin and sees the high-glinting polish of the wooden skin. The musical voice is calm and warm, a little sleepy at this time of the morning, though Kate has been sitting waiting for the telephone to sound its double ring. She says, "Hel-*lo*!" in welcome, as though she knows that it can be no one but Marj, and Marj's cells do their quick change, recharged with happiness.

They will never quarrel, they tell each other. They will be able to discuss everything; it has always been Kate's deep belief that differences can be solved by patience and the power of reason. "I irritate people," Marj writes, "I explain them to themselves and get carried away." Kate answers, "I'll know you so well that you won't feel the need to irritate me." They have been, with love in their hearts, preparing a map for disagreement: this is where you begin, where you diverge at the fork of the road, the moment when each takes a different road. Then somehow they are facing each other and collide before there is time to stop. At first the collisions are cushioned by the distance between continents and Kate's unmistakable silences on the telephone, caused, Marj will learn, by the wind going out of her.

"I'll know you so well," not "You'll know me so well." Kate will anticipate Marj's need to irritate and direct a scene in which it is deflected. We yearn to be known, but only on our own terms? In our own language, perhaps with a precious remnant of dishonesty? At love's beginning the lovers are twin transparencies; they exchange the fine material of their identities. It is the time of dazzling intuitions and conspiracies of agreement. Marj, lighter than air, exhales Kate's love, she wants to spread her glad news of the miracle, the love between two old women who live on different continents, who have never met. "It's a long-distance love story!" she says to Marianne, her friend for thirty-one years. They have survived illusions and quarrels; they confide in each other in a place of careful friendship on the far side of anger. Marianne pricks up her ears. "She's like you," Marj says, "a lover of life. She dances, she sings, she likes brandy and soda. She's the kind of woman you love." "Oh, I know I'm going to fall in love with her," Marianne says joyfully. She tells friends how lucky Marj is to be loved by this life-loving woman. She reads Kate's handwriting. "She has a marvellous clear mind, she is both proud and insecure, she's kind, she's so kind." Their friends are allies now, for Kate comes alive through Marianne, through her photographs, through the complicity of intuition, astrology and runes; Kate's essence instantly takes shape in Marianne, the novelist, and her friends. Via Marianne's vision of Kate, the friends know that Kate is charming, beautiful, witty, terribly intelligent. "What about her voice?" asks Marj. "Her voice," says Marianne, "séduisante."

The planets and the runes are insistently on Kate's side. Kate has sought counsel on her relationship with Marj, and fishes out the Horse, the rune of Movement, of Progress. "You have progressed far enough to feel a measure of safety in your position. It is time to turn again and face the future reassured. The sharing is significant since it relates to the sun's power to foster life and illumi-nates all things with its light." Annie, the astrologist, gazing at Kate's chart on her computer, sees Kate's ascen-dant between Scorpio and Sagittarius. "That's why she's so passionate!" she explains. "She analyzes everything. She can talk a lot without saying exactly what she thinks. She has an artist's temperament. Her self-control comes from will power but she doesn't know how to control her emotions." Annie keeps some of the evidence to herself, just hints at the vulnerability that tips Kate into a depression where no dialogue is possible.

Marj notices that in her letters Kate takes out insurance policies against disappointment. Unnecessary defences against possible criticism. Every joy must be tempered by caution. She is looking at herself as she dances to the tape of *Cabaret*: "Boring? Funny? Tragi-comic?" she writes to Marj. Just in case, she turns to face an enemy. "I'm only a 'sort-of' writer!...too tired, too easily diverted." She was, she says, a good teacher, "promoting young talent instead of my own? *But did I have any?* I've always needed quite a lot of solitude and that's when I've written my best stuff...IN MY HEAD." She strikes down her own confidence, which takes its shadow—doubt. Its doppelgänger. She is writing an autobiographical novel, she says, about a woman named Frances. Frances, too, is paralyzed by doubt; she knows "failures and tantrums." Kate looks at her mirror image with wry humour. Part of Marj's hubris is her belief that she can give Kate the confidence that life keeps draining out of her. Kate's repeated runnings-down of herself are all part of a ritual dance, Marj says to herself—of preparation for their meeting. She herself, along with her showing-off, as she calls it, has issued some warnings: that she looks older than Kate's image of her; that she is relatively unpractised in the art of love, that Kate, who is deep and thorough, and can recite reams of poetry by heart, will discover her "lacunae." The word "lacunae" makes her shake with irrepressible laughter.

Kate sends Marj a photograph of herself. Marj examines it with a magnifying glass, studies the white hair that frames Kate's face, gossamer-fine, brushed back from the forehead. The head is tilted and Kate's questioning look seems to ask, "Who am I? Do you like what you see? I come empty-handed and I am sad and uncertain about myself." A vertical line between the high arched eyebrows, one more arched than the other, speaks of love's ironies, the fluctuating balance between giver and receiver, of love unspent and love ungiven. In a second photograph, taken for a passport, Marj recognizes the same look in the woman forty years younger, with dark eyebrows and dark hair. The higher-arched right eyebrow is drawn emphatically, the eyes look beyond the photographer, the mouth is the perfect mouth of late Greek sculpture, of an athletic youth, proud and tenderly sensual. Kate, on the brink of the unknown, is going to England to seek her fortune. "*Is* your expression yearning?" Marj asks her on the telephone. Kate thinks back; was there someone at whom her mind's eyes were looking, a face out there beyond the photographer, that she yearned to see? She was worried about her leap into space without a penny, she says.

"Do you think I look a little like Constance?" Kate has written on the back of her first photograph, and Marj answers, "Yes, you do look like Constance, with the same kind of indestructible beauty." Kate has seen both Constance and Marj on the screen: a friend has remarked to her that they look alike. They have the same high-nosed, imperial profile and ageless skin, the same conquering look that Helen of Troy must have had. Their faces, too, have launched ships, on a more modest and less deadly scale. And in surprising ways, perhaps for the same reasons, they are alike. Both had fathers burdened by secrets that the family struggled to hide and protect. Both of them, brought up in the bosom of churches, lost their faith in God, and both have a hankering nostalgia for the pageantry of the church ritual. Both lost their faith in themselves: Constance when she was still young; Kate, after years when she was at one with her charisma, brilliant in her work and secure in love, suffered a series of blows to her ego and a bout of paralyzing doubt. Like Constance's doubt? I am nothing. Behind the nothingness both felt was a fierce sense of: I *am* something, and an accumulating anger turning inward.

Marj makes a composite portrait from the batch of photographs that arrive—Kate Now. Here she is standing in
the terraced garden below her apartment, against a backdrop of hibiscus in full scarlet bloom; her hands are
clasped in front of her, her smile beams kindness. Marj
commits to memory Kate's radiantly healthy face, her
strong and delicate hands, narrow hips and small feet,
shod in ankle-height boots, her striped black and white
cardigan and pink turtleneck shirt. She constructs one of
her scenarios, an exactly imagined rehearsal for a time
shortly after their meeting, their vibrating intensity of
touch and the pas de deux hands that will never say, what
do we do next? She runs her second finger over the high
crescent of Kate's right eyebrow, along the snowy hairline
down to the hollow in front of her ear, and then, if Kate
obligingly keeps her mouth open in a smile, traces the
step down that her right front tooth makes before it joins
the others. Just at this imaginary moment Kate's teeth
close as gently on Marj's thumb as a mother alligator's do
when she positions one of her hatchlings to safety in her
mouth.

Marj practises her imaging wherever she goes. Her eyes
fasten on a woman in the supermarket or on the street;
something about her reminds Marj of her idea of Kate;
perhaps it is the decided way the woman walks and her
white hair, ruffled by the wind. The woman always has a
healthy, sun-browned face and a confident air; sometimes
she is standing in line at the bank and Marj scrutinizes
her; sometimes the woman speaks, graciously (she has
seen Marj in the film) but coolly, since Marj, with Kate in
her mind, has become a mite too friendly. Or even a little
rude? For Marj sometimes stares so hard at women who
remind her of Kate that they think that she knows them,
or that they know her. She is happy when the most
promising look-alike is a friend of friends; she is small
and impetuous and listens to Marj's love story with

infectious merriment. She could be Kate's younger sister, thinks Marj. At a future time, she and Kate will meet and appraise each other, and the friend will say, "We don't look alike, but you look very much like my mother."

"The obsession that is (or isn't?) love," Kate writes. Benign or dangerous? It dictates the quality of days, shortens or lengthens, darkens or brightens them, charges the mind with manic high spirits and reckless laughter. It coats the soul with wicked equanimity toward the horrors of life. Unfeeling, or an imbalance of feeling; it is an over-grown garden in full flower, fed by laughter that bubbles from its centre. The backlash comes with a vision of some transcendent wrong that focusses the misery of the world into a single burning-point.

Marj, in her state of headlong joy, is brought up short by the story told by a woman journalist who has just come back from Somalia. She watched the burial, she says, of a child who has died of starvation. As he was being lowered into a grave dug out of the desert sand, she saw him open his eyes, she saw a tear roll out of each eye.

I've been tranquillized, Marj thinks. She is no longer the pre-love self who mourned daily the outrages committed by the human race and denounced those who committed them. She is unable to feel angry or even impatient. She holds the perilous belief that she and Kate are sufficient unto themselves; together they will make their love into a work of art as they live it. For they are old and wise and experienced, aren't they? In the course of her life Marj has made precipitous leaps into the unknown and has gleaned from them, if not always happiness, at least useful knowl-edge about life and love. The leap she has been mulling over is the greatest and the most daring. She will go to Australia.

They have been moving toward each other so rapidly that the only space left to cross is the geographical space between them. "You *should* think seriously of coming here for a *visit!?*" writes Kate. She has written Marj about the converging of omens, and destiny's insistent hints; now she describes her apartment with its view of Sydney Harbour, and the "waterside park *immediately* below me—there are trees and some birds—and I'm quite a good cook. (*Am* I?)" She "would want it to be absolutely wonderful," and the thought makes her nervous. They will meet; it will be the once and for all meeting between imagination and reality. Marj has no fear of this, it will be exactly like their scenarios, the imagined has become real in their pre-meeting, their long mutual introduction. They are ruled by destiny at the heart of being, their certainties indivisibly include the future. But the thought of the trip terrifies Marj. "The trip is bloody awful," an Australian friend tells her. "The trip is murder, but when you get off the plane you feel Australian energy rising right through your feet." Then, unexpectedly, comes the sudden transfusion of confidence, and Marj hears herself say to friends, "I'm going to Australia." They do not seem surprised; they have known people who have gone to Australia and come back, too. But some of them have misgivings: it doesn't always work out the way you think it will. What if you don't like each other? It's hard to explain why they are both so certain. "Of course we'll like each other!" Haven't they talked about the dangers? "You've analyzed so profoundly the pitfalls of my visit," says Marj, "its most extreme potential for separating us." There are affirmative voices, too. "Of course I'm *delighted* that you're going to Australia," writes Marj's painter friend who had hitchhiked alone in Africa when she was seventy-five. "Isn't it exciting that life gets better and better as you get older?" She is eighty-nine now, she paints better than ever, she is radiant with the blaze of her spirit. She writes on the envelope, "Let me know about the Old Age Epiphanies as they go along."

Now, secure in the confidence of a meeting, they leap to the future beyond it, when each will be incapable of living without the other. Will one of them change continents, and which will it be? Kate loves problem-solving; she tackles this one by making a list of possibilities, with advantages and disadvantages in separate columns. Marj, in imagination, leaps from the British Isles to a mid-point island in the South Pacific, sees herself and Kate somewhere in eternal summer or in an imprecise, bone-chilling winter; she looks at a screen in her mind and calls up an image: two women, sick with nostalgia, have turned against each other. "It's your fault!" each cries. They are engaged in bitter warfare. No more moving, says Marj to herself. In the course of her life she has changed continents twice. We are old, she thinks, we are rooted in the ground of Australia and North America, in the elements and the seasons, even in the position of the sun, the moon and the constellations.

Marj is rooted in her friends and in her work. And Kate's trips to Canada have ended with a sense of disappointment and alienation, and a horror of snowbound winter. Everything can be worked out, Marj thinks, in the context of their staying right where they are. "We mustn't build on unreal hopes," she writes Kate.

How hard, how chilling Marj's certainty is! It leaves no room at all for Kate's hopes or for the exercise of her powers of persuasion. "We might think of living in England," she says on the telephone. Marj answers, "I don't want to live in England." Silence. One of Kate's silences. Then she says, "I can dream, can't I?" Kate is staking out her space of dreaming; she wants Marj to enter it, to roam there with her freely, and Marj refuses to set foot in it. Is this her profound yielding of autonomy?

What exactly are you going to sacrifice in the name of love? Your time? Your space? Your home? Is Kate thinking of Marj's joking suggestion for a title: *With Holdings?* Their book? Midway between the generosity of love and the stinginess of self. A portrait of Marj? Kate sees that the question of autonomy is by no means solved, that it can only be solved by fruitful negotiating sessions when they meet. By then she will know Marj so well that she won't need to fall into any of her old habits; she will need neither to be irritating nor to withhold. Between the two of them it will be all holdings. Suddenly, Marj sees Kate as Liza, singing at the top of her lungs with the leaping and plunging rhythm of the song, "Lady peaceful, lady happy, that's what I want to be!"

"I *have* wondered about our meeting—and the pain of separation," Kate writes. "And the distance again, but I still want that meeting…. It's as though we've known each other for ages and at the same time it has the elation of new love." Marj tells Kate that she is teaching her the real meaning of love. Their thoughts are dancing together again, the dance of multiple veils, the two of them alone in a magic circle of light. They will meet; the imagined will become real. They write pre-meeting scenarios: "the sudden privacy of the car," says Kate, "eyes meeting eyes in wonder…the touch of hands. That moment of seeing…and touching." They both see themselves being seen—by a "surprised truck driver high in his cabin, catching a glimpse"; he takes his story "home to the wife," says Kate. "We don't say hello," says Marj, "We may not say anything at all; we may just embrace in a decorous and formal way; we may walk in silence to your little car; you may say, 'I'll just put your bags in the boot.' And, seated on your right-hand driver's side, you'll take a quick look-around and say, 'Marj?' And I may take your hands and kiss them…. Or there may be some big Australian grazier just getting into the pick-up truck next to us and looking down on you with lascivious connivance." Marianne has her scenario, too. "She will see you before you see her," she says. At the Sydney Airport, she means. It will happen: Kate will have her back against a wall, will be leaning outward, scanning the passengers as they come out, pushing their baggage-wagons. Marj will see a white head, a parrot profile turned toward her; at this point the real Kate will once and for all displace the imagined one, and in the second of her hesitation, Marj will read, "Are you disappointed?" Is she waiting with sudden anxiety for Marj to make the first move? "Would Madam like a taxi?" Their laughter—of joyful relief—will echo the scenarios, in the moment when imagination is transformed into reality. People will smile at the two white-haired elders, at their repeated hugging, while Marj, the taller one, will plant kisses on every handy part of Kate's head, and they will go off, carrying Marj's bags with their free hands, while each wraps a possessive arm around her new-old friend.

Chapter Two

In the pre-time being, in the rehearsal period for the real, Marj wrote to Kate, "I've been doing exercises between visible and invisible, between imagining touch and really touching." Each created her scenario, synchronized gestures and responses, and the melting of one imagined body into the other. At the moment of meeting they are not surprised by the alchemy that instantly changes imagination into reality. They don't say a word; Marj's senses are doing the talking, whispering the delight that rushes along her arm around Kate's shoulders. Their two dissimilar bodies recognize a long, predetermined assent. They are speeding away from the airport in Kate's little car; Marj's right hand closes over Kate's small, sunburned left hand. "If your left hand is on the gearshift," she had written, "will you practise turning it over briefly so that I can kiss your palm?" Kate releases her hand to change gears and slides her thumb into the valley of Marj's palm. "Hello, my darling," she says. She is looking intently at the road, squinting into the sun with narrowed blue-gleaming eyes; her hand stretches out to come lightly to rest on Marj's thigh. They drive into the sunny courtyard of Kate's apartment building and stop at one of the entrances, flanked by flowering oleanders in big terra-cotta pots. A lean grey and white cat, Kate's cat, Oliver, comes to twine around her legs. Kate fixes him with a hypnotic stare, moves her hands in lazy wave-motion over his head; his jade eyes gaze back at her, his body weaves to her hands' rhythm and to her murmuring cat-talk. Then he leads them upstairs to the door of Kate's apartment. "We will drop my bags just inside the door," wrote Marj in her pre-meeting scenario. They drop the bags, silently look each other up and down with a serious, confirming look, and kiss each other with delicate greed.

In Marj's scenario, the first meeting with its impetuous embraces was suspended in the question: and after that? Will they move toward a bed, fall on it and engage in passionate love-play? Kate was able to imagine, better than Marj, the reality of two white-haired strangers meeting. "Perhaps I'll put you to bed," she wrote. "And let you sleep," she added with brisk good sense. Her schedule for today, already planned, holds a nap for Marj, a walk down to the harbour's edge, lunchtime, teatime and drinkie-time, when each will toast the other, looking lovingly over her glass of brandy and soda. She has already made sandwiches and prepared a casserole. Before they met, Marj scarcely dared believe that they would feel so instantly comfortable together, and that now, standing just inside the shelter of the closed door, their anterior life would compel them to touch with this eager familiarity, or this hunger for more. They stand for a moment at arms' length, swaying to the inaudible music of delight. "You must be tired, darling," says Kate. "We must get you settled." Their hands slacken and drop, and Kate leads Marj into the shipshape room that looks over the gleam and dazzle of the harbour. Like an obedient child, Marj puts herself into Kate's care, yields to her sense of timing. There is plenty of time to linger in the exciting place between desire and fulfillment, where passion burns with a steady flame; they will stay here for a while before they venture on to the less certain ground of lovemaking. They will improvise every few minutes on the theme of embraces and deep kisses.

They are on Kate's stage, in Kate's theatre. "It must all be perfect," wrote Kate to Marj, and the skills of a lifetime have gone into the preparations for Marj's arrival. Kate has cleared out her own room and squeezed everything under the bed and on upper shelves of the little room across the hall. Instead of Marj's splendid view of the harbour, Kate sees only the leaves of a tree just outside her high window. Marj luxuriates in Kate's space and view and is happy to accept Kate's denials that her life has been turned upside down to make Marj comfortable. She and Kate love each other too much, Marj thinks, to get on each other's nerves. She reverently contemplates the few clothes that Kate has left at one end of the closet, and a tidy platoon of colourful sandals and moccasins drawn up below.

By the end of their first day together, Kate has caught a whiff of Marj's austere discipline. She is terribly polite. She likes to eat but cannot be wheedled into eating an ounce more than she wants. She is indifferent to the rite of drinkie-time. She even oversees the pouring of her drink; fourteen drops of brandy, she stipulates, only partly joking.

But Marj has never felt less austere, and is entranced by the flesh-and-blood Kate, who, in the middle of dinner, puts on a tape of *Cabaret* and sings, high-kicking her way from living room to kitchen. She turns a joyful face back toward Marj, her eyes flash blue, she blows Marj a kiss, and holds out her arms in an invitation to Marj to dance. Marj has already imagined this—how their bodies would lock together; her sure sense of the hills and hollows of Kate's body against her own is enough to send tremors coursing through her. How gracefully she glided around her kitchen when she danced with Kate in imagination! Now her feet stumble and step on Kate's feet, and Marj almost loses her balance. They both stop. "You'd better just do your own thing," Kate says. Kate will tell Marj that she danced as soon as she toddled; her mother held her upstretched hands and bounced her little feet up and down. "Dance-a-baby-did-it!" her mother sang and Kate shouted her glee. What ecstasy at school to place her warm hand on a schoolmate's waist and draw her close into a magic circle. Now she is looking at Marj coolly—as the adjudicator, Marj thinks, the dispenser of impartial justice. Marj wants to apologize for her self-conscious body suddenly aware of its own awkwardness, longing for another chance. But she has failed two tests today: she can't drink, she can't dance. And Kate's inscrutable look, new to Marj, seems to say, "It's too late to teach you how to dance. But I want you to learn *me*. Are you capable of learning me?" Marj will happily learn Kate. And aren't they dancing together in another way as they move up the scale of before-play? They will know soon, when the day will have a single unstated purpose, when its beginning will make haste slowly toward the end—lovemaking, how the end will suffuse the day with tenderness.

Today is that day. Marj opens the patio door of her room and looks out at the broad, white-gold stripe the sun casts on the water, and on its blinding reflection in the windowpanes of a distant skyscraper. The cloudless day has begun to warm up. Across the water, the bow of a robin's-egg blue container ship with a yellow funnel and cranes is being pulled sideways by an invisible tug, and in no time tugs appear at bow and stern to coax the ship close to the quay. After breakfast, Kate and Marj race downhill to catch the ferry; it arrives at the dock in a flurry of foam, of waves splashing on the rocks, and then lies waiting, trembling to take off again. "Hello darling!" Kate says to the woman who takes their tickets, launching her whole body forward like the Winged Victory. It is an example of her singular gift for instant seduction: she can bale up a stranger, wrap someone in sheer charm, as fast as a spider can package a fly. They make for the upper front bench and sit pressed together; their hands are clasped with interwoven fingers in the warm crevice between their bodies. Kate is in her reckless state, she seems to be saying to the whole world, "Look at us. We love each other!" Contagious love that enters into the astonishments and epiphanies of the day.

They disembark at Circular Quay and join the throng in the unending promenade; people look at their joyful faces and smile back. A space is cleared for a family of wound-up toy pandas toddling across the quay. Sacred ibises stroll along, stiff-legged; their long curved beaks snatch up bits of fallen bread, potato chips, ice cream cones; they sidestep with a flutter of wings as Kate and Marj sweep by arm-in-arm. Kate is an Australian microcosm; people step gladly into the sunshine and blue sky of her embracing laugh which animates her entire body, which can set off the incredible merriment of babies in their strollers and bewitch their moms. Her laugh says, "Come, I'll show you how to be happy." She invites people to laugh by imitation, just as she invites Oliver, the cat, to dance, hypnotized by the movement of her two hands and the weaving of her body.

Now it is evening and Kate, entering Marj's room, leaves the door partly open, with a light beyond in the corridor, diffused to twilight around Marj's single bed. She pulls the shades down over the two halves of the patio door, over the intrusive lights from the street: headlights rounding the corner and coming up the hill past the apartment, harbour lights, bright ribbons of colour reflected in the black water, big lamps on the dock where the container ship is tethered. So love's space is a single bed bounded by a book-covered table on one side, a small desk on the other, a bureau, a chair with Marj's clothes lying tidily on it. This is their circumference, with

32

the soft bed at the centre, silky sheets, a pillow for each, edged with a fluted ruffle. With due modesty, they have taken off pyjamas (Marj), a nightgown (Kate), and Kate on one elbow is looking down at Marj. "You are beautiful," she says. Marj in the twilight half-sees the pale rise of her hip turned toward Kate. They are young, they are going to make love with the lithe movements of youth, they will forget the daytime facts of age, their young faces will approach each other. Kate's eyes are half-closed; the blue glance, the chiselled lips, the slightly longer tooth are tenderly revealed. Marj has barely time to think, how can you look so young, and what makes this glimpse of tooth so enchanting? when their mouths, passionately meeting, engage in a sinuous dance of tongues, each with a fore-knowledge of response, for these kisses happened before they met and have happened since their meeting. It is likely to happen whenever they meet, even across the dining room table, and to cause them to look at each other with surprise. "I thought you wrote, 'Old age will save me from desire in its usual sense,'" said Kate on one of these occasions. "Oh yes, so I did," Marj said, "but I didn't know." Know the strange magnetism of a body accepted, much more natural and accepted than her own flesh. Nor the tug toward the strong, knowing, uninsistent hands that draw their bodies together. Together they seem like flocking birds or fish who know when to turn in unison, to rise, to wheel or sink to earth or water. The consenting, identical flight, dark or pale, suddenly flashing. Lovemaking. "We both know that it will happen," Marj wrote to Kate, after months of skirting around the subject in their letters.

Now it is happening, though Kate has wisely set the stage, for there is a shade of anxiety in each; each knows about the watershed of sex, about the impossibility of ever going back to the innocent passion of sex-suspended. They know that desire is unpredictable and that its captious temperament is tied to egos and self-esteems. They have written each other about the dangers and vowed to keep their sense of humour, no matter what, thinking to foresee and outwit the traps of either success or failure. "I've been told that I love splendidly," wrote Kate. Now their interlaced bodies spread molten heat, share tension and shudders of delight. Orgasm, when the body bursts its bounds with a glad cry. "Orgasms are not compulsory," Kate wrote before they met, and Marj laughed with foreknowledge. Not compulsory but inevitable. How could they have thought for a minute that they would not need this as the affirmation of their embodied life together? They are lovers now. Will they look at each other differently? Do they know each other better, now that they know how their hands and mouths can wander over the unfamiliar landscape of a new body, restlessly moving like a new world in formation? Now that they know how the hands, the mouth can greet and take possession of uprising nipples, and move confidently down, deep into a widening valley, and bathe in a warm flood of welcome?

Each is newly known and unknown to the other, each is exploring a new world with old maps, has suddenly urgent questions about wants and needs. Each is learning new inflections of yes, no, here, there, now, shades of silence. When it dares, the English language timidly translates a universe of signs. There are presages at the heart of their lovely closeness: for Marj, old beginnings with their endings, like a crescent moon holding the old moon in her arms; for Kate, fear, its long shadow over her life. Next morning she takes the two pillows which Marj has placed side by side on her bed and puts one on top of the other. "Pillows side by side suggest two people," she says with a little laugh. As if to say, "I know you understand these silly niceties; you, too, have lived through the Terror."

"We are lovers now." Marj likes this momentous phrase. Later, when she is back in Canada, a friend who has done her own imagining will ask, "Did you make love?" "Of course you'll make love," she had predicted. Marj was wary. "It's under discussion," she said. Post facto, she will smile—a smile tinted with the old ineradicable guilt and, because she is seventy-five, a small new fear—that she will provoke smiles herself.

But it is this day, this day after, and Marj inhabits her new-old body uncritically, spreads herself from the inside out, freed from her ingrown imagination which has exaggerated the sharpness of her bones and the irreversible signs of old age. Their two dissimilar bodies, impalpable as warm summer air, passion-laden, have met and merged; their gestures in slow motion have found each other by echolocation, each the mirror of the other. They have played the love scene according to their imaginary rehearsals which left plenty of room for improvisation. Kate, an old hand at directing love scenes in the theatre, has felt the responsibility of getting this one right—a scene between two old women, who, by daylight, are as modest as nuns. From their first day together they seemed to have agreed wordlessly to identical rules of etiquette, which required each to dress, to undress, in the privacy of her room. Their love-repertoire, which could be resumed spontaneously, was suspended, apparently by mutual consent, just short of lovemaking.

Today contains subliminal messages about the correct position of pillows. Prudence will dictate Kate's wariness with friends, a necessary blurring, she thinks, of the great truth which Marj wants to announce to the world. Marj would like to take a megaphone and shout over the harbour, "Kate and I are lovers!" The harbour amplifies sound and spreads light into every corner of Marj's room. Diamonds of light sparkle on the water. Kate is in the kitchen, giving Oliver his breakfast, and Marj, under her potent spell, understands that today, too, has its time-table. There are possibilities for interruption: the plaintive mewing of Oliver, a ring of the doorbell or the telephone, an eruption of furious barking in the street below and the anguished cries of Miss Muffet, dressed from head to paws in beige curls. She is pelting down the street (everybody who has a view has appeared at windows or on balconies) just ahead of her persecutors, a nondescript pair whose dearest wish is to tear Miss Muffet to pieces. In the rear Janet waves her arms and shouts. By now Kate in her peignoir is hanging over the balcony railing and Janet, under hypnosis, it seems, looks up, and her fierce look fades. Her eyes are as blue as Kate's; if her look is fierce it is because life never tires of tormenting her with its dirty tricks; for solace she has a big calico cat and the two dogs, Horace and Frank. Today, Miss Muffet, swift as a wind-driven tumbleweed, will outstrip the others and they will wearily climb the hill and bend their heads while Janet fastens on their leashes. On other days, Miss Muffet is caught unawares and pandemonium breaks out in the courtyard, the entire population of the apartment house spills out, shouts, waves canes…. But this is today, any today with glorious sunshine, and for Kate and Marj, there are no urgent engagements.

Are they different today? Has their new knowledge, each of each, changed them? Questions have been born that need not be asked; they are part of the immediate guesswork of lovemaking. Some contain the fear of answers; they are written in invisible ink, will appear palely when Kate's disappointment rewrites the love scene. On the day after, Marj floats in lightness and she is sure of her body's power to wake Kate's body, which, however, follows its daytime schedule with a firm baseline of motherly briskness and order. For Kate is not going to be distracted from her plan for the day, even when Marj, wearing Kate's blue velvet dressing-gown, comes up behind her in the kitchen, clasps her arms around Kate's waist, moves her hands up over Kate's breasts. Kate's stillness seems an eternity to Marj, who will reconstruct this moment two years later in her search for clues. Kate has turned gently and is looking Marj up and down, from her white head to her bare feet. "It looks nice on you," she says. It is the first of her invitations to Marj to wear her, to play her part, it is a bit of theatre that will bring about a communion of identities. Marj, who has a lifelong habit of dressing for breakfast, even in her love-states, now feels the touch of velvet against her skin, the warm morning air that caresses her in the gaps between buttons. The dressing-gown falls on either side of her legs when she stretches out her feet to touch Kate's under the table. It is breakfast time and Kate will begin to recount the story of her life.

They would write a book together, "which should have joy as its essence," Marj wrote Kate before they met, "because we love each other *that* much. It will be our love-flowering, it will be called *The Time Being*. Each of us will keep her voice." Kate answered, "Our book, *The Time Being*—I like the juxtaposition of tenderness and passion." And Marj answered Kate, "We'll have such good discussions—what to put into our book and what to leave out." In a dream she saw two books, close together in a single block; their titles were *Truth* and *Real*. Those are our two voices, she thought; they will separate and merge, they will merge at the moment of our meeting. They will follow our bodies' rhythms. She wrote to Kate, "I hope you know that you're the only person in the course of my life that I've wanted to write a book with." She confided her idea to friends, some of whom murmured their doubts. But Marj knew that it was possible; hadn't it been accomplished by four of her friends, two lesbian couples, four gifted poets who loved each other that much, who had interwoven their voices and created a single-double identity? Yet even before she met Kate, Marj's vision of indivisibility was a bit clouded. "Each of us will keep her voice?" Even then perhaps she was more possessive of her voice than any of her four poet-friends. And of her thoughts? Marj and Kate will merge in the time of mutual candour, when Kate is recounting her life with the conviction that it will be safe in Marj's mind, that Marj will neither add to nor subtract from it. They started continents apart and are meeting now at the intersection of an X. They begin to move apart at the point where they meet. Kate will renounce any part in the writing of the book, and will come to think of the gift of her life story with sick regret.

Kate hauls from hiding two scrapbooks bulging with the stuff of her life: photographs, clippings, ticket stubs, theatre programs, reviews and newspaper articles. Details hold Kate's history fixed in time and place. She notices right away how careless Marj is about the correct ordering of time; Kate can tell her repeatedly what year she went to England to seek her fortune, what year she went to Canada; the dates slide over Marj's mind and vanish. Later Kate will write down the main events of her life in chronological order to stabilize Marj, who appears to be lost in speculation about lovers, how they met, why they broke up. Marj tries to discern patterns; Kate sees Marj's patterns as a threat to her autonomy. Had Kate left or had the other woman left, Marj wonders. And what about the love affair that never happened—with so-and-so who "would have liked a bit of a skiffle," or so-and-so who said when she first laid eyes on Kate, "Oh no, not that again!" Twenty years later, with Marj in Canada, Kate will dream about this woman, whose hair, dyed pink like spun sugar in the dream, is piled up in a beehive. Kate in the dream is going back to a school commencement; she has to give a speech. She thinks of saying, "I'm glad to be back in the place where I spent so many happy hours," but she has not prepared her speech and is seized by panic. The place where she was happy was her boarding school, St. Anne's, the place of charisma, of honours, of her first great love. Kate will puzzle over the meaning of this dream; Marj will suggest an interpretation. "It's about the ordeal of coming to Canada," she says.

Marj is contemplating a photograph of a beautiful woman and has confused the order of Kate's lovers. "No, that was before I went to England," Kate says patiently. Marj cares less about dates than about the thousands of fine strands that have woven the shining web of Kate's life. She looks avidly at the photographs of Kate and her friends standing in the sunshine; she wants to be a young woman with the others. She loves the seductive Kate whose dark eyebrows arch high above her half-closed eyes, she loves Kate's laughing mouth. She looks both confident and sceptical. She is holding a long-haired cat under each arm. Now she gives Marj the names and curricula vitae of all the cats who shared this part of her life. "You look like Barbara Stanwyck," says Marj. "They used to tell me I looked like Ava Gardner," says Kate. Marj stares at the women who compose Kate's memories of life and love. Some of them are teachers, one works in the theatre, one is a musician. They are at home in their minds and bodies, they share professional passwords and the authority teachers and directors need to restore order. They have disciplined schedules for work; they know how to run a household, what days to do the washing and ironing and shopping, how to plan meals and cook them and make a shopping list without forgetting a single necessary item. They love parties and booze and rousing arguments which end in a chivalrous spirit in which they raise their visors and lower their spears. "You know, you may be right," Kate quotes one of them as saying at the end of one of these evenings. Marj feels envious.

Kate is looking at Marj with the cool shock of recognition of their ill-fated dance together. "You've never had to work for a living, have you?" "Well, there was my teaching job, and then the Navy," Marj says. "But you've never *had* to work for a living." No, Marj has never known the anxiety of looking for a job, the necessity of keeping it; she has never lived in poverty. This is a big defect, she thinks humbly, as bad as never having known motherhood. Kate has never known motherhood either but she knows all about babies. They stop crying when they look at her; they begin to laugh. One of her many jobs, she tells Marj, was as a live-in nanny; she taught a young mother to get over her terror of her infant son. Kate laid her cheek against his navel. "It's a boozle baby," she crooned, "it's a baby boozle baby thing," and the baby laughed in delight.

The Kate who looked like Ava Gardner went to England to seek her fortune. She was the Kate of the passport photograph with the yearning eyes. She joined a repertory theatre, travelled to every corner of England, acted, stage-managed, directed. It was during the golden age of British theatre; Kate's theatre programs are studded with the names of those who were to become Dames and Knights of the British Empire. She had soaked up her theatrical knowledge from her actor father, who quit the theatre for the church. "My father drank too much and made my mother unhappy," says Kate. "I look like my mother." She shows Marj a photograph of her mother, almost her twin, with the same arched nose and heavy-lidded blue eyes. Kate inherited her mother's face, and her mother's "Pollyanna side," along with her father's flexible body and intellect, quick-flaring temper (Marj will learn), the changes he could ring on himself, the ability to act, for which Marj feels spellbound admiration. Theatre people have always struck fear into her; mockery lies just below their surface, for they have uncanny powers of observation and imitation. Kate's father had the soul and charisma of a great actor; he transformed his services into theatre. In the hush of the darkened church, he dropped his melodious voice almost to a whisper: "Lighten our darkness, oh Lord" (Kate's voice is a musical pianissimo), "and by thy Grace defend us from the perils of the night." Kate's father, who chose all the colours and materials of the vestments, and directed the lighting of the church, bequeathed to Kate his artistic gifts, along with the versatile instrument of his lungs.

But—"he made my mother unhappy," Kate said. Those matchless lungs that Kate inherited "shouted and accused," Kate wrote in a poem she showed Marj. He had drunk too much wine; the faint smell of it pervaded the vicarage. Sometimes he declaimed a great scene from *King Lear* or *Timon of Athens*. Timon, the too-generous king who felt let down by the entire world, was one of the Reverend's favourite heroes. "The unkindest beast is kinder than mankind!" he cried out to Button, the old family dog, who had, at an opportune moment, climbed into the Reverend's chair. "Button to the woods!" he shouted, while Button wagged his tail and rolled his eyes uneasily.

Kate's father "shouted and accused." He struck histrionic poses; he said that no one understood him nor knew how hard it was to be a man of God, while his wife sat silently and Button crept out of the room. Kate, a child of six, was watching; she had witnessed the same scene many times, she loyally kept the family secret but her heart had hardened.

Now Marj stares at a photograph of Kate as a child. She has a big adult head, a grave, enquiring expression, which is not in the least childlike. Kate has also dug out a worn piece of paper typed on both sides—the analysis by an itinerant phrenologist named Cedric Pond of the bumps of

Kate's six-year-old head. He was made welcome at the vicarage and encouraged to read the heads of the entire family. Marj imagines him as a small bearded man in a black suit, with delicate blue-veined hands. He is looking at Kate, whose pale eyes are focussed on him appraisingly, her mouth slightly open (he notices the gleam of a tooth). Her body is comfortably relaxed, standing on thin, sturdy legs. Her head makes him think of a full moon, with its mountains and craters in pale-gold sunlight. Mr. Pond cups his hands over the top of this head where the fine hair is smoothly combed, and he reads its surface with his thumbs and sensitive forefingers, with closed eyes, while his lips move. In his near-trance he has a sense of playing Kate's head, of bringing forth sublime music; he is moved almost to tears. In his forty-five years of practice he has never been so enchanted.

"She is a born thinker of a high order," Mr. Pond will write after the seance, "with a great grasp of principle—an insatiable desire to know the 'why and wherefore' of things. Logical, far-seeing." The bumps vibrate with messages. He reads only a few gentle warnings: "Her chief urge will come from the desire for distinction which is very strong." "She is even of nature...slow to make up her mind; firm to obstinacy when she has...a very deep sense of humour.... Her planning power and general fertility of resource is amazing." Marj has a sense of awe as she reads; she has conjured up the scene sixty-three years ago—a six-year-old child standing in front of a small grey-bearded man with his eyes closed and his extra-sensory hands moving over her head. "Somewhat highly sexed" (Marj reads Mr. Pond's analysis out loud), "but the pitfalls are avoided by both balances—the prudential and the moral." Marj bursts out with a delighted laugh. "Hmm, I wonder," says Kate. "She can be a great teacher," Marj reads, "especially of the Grammar School type. She will enter public life in some fashion as leader, speaker and writer. The urge is in her."

Mr. Pond's hands move and pause; his thumbs have touched the bump of sensitivity; his index fingers, like a moth's antennae, explore its "ill-effects...almost purely subjective." He has discovered the same danger in all the family heads: destructive emotions and feelings of worth-lessness. He opens his eyes on the child standing in front of him. Cheeky, though; that will protect her, he thinks, looking keenly at her head, tipped now, and at her faintly mocking lips.

"She will enter public life in some fashion as leader, speaker and writer," wrote Mr. Pond. Marj has come to the breakfast table with a notebook and pencil. Kate will tell her about Theresa Graham, who taught diction at St. Anne's, Kate's boarding school, who moulded Kate to fit Mr. Pond's vision, though she was unaware both of Mr. Pond and of the sibylline piece of paper Marj now has in front of her. Miss Graham infused the teaching of diction with passionate energy; it meant the correct speaking of words; it meant a thorough knowledge of drama, its practice and theory. Like Cedric Pond, Theresa Graham immediately recognized Kate's gifts, she felt her own power to shape this fourteen-year-old girl who seemed to absorb the intensities of words, the precise delicacies of meaning through the pores of her skin. She liked to look at Kate's schoolgirl face and into the eyes, moonstone colour or the colour of reef water, that were fixed on her with unnerving attention. She liked Kate's arching eyebrows and decisively modelled lips, unconsciously sensual, too, and challenging. When teachers and students, students and students, danced together after supper to a wind-up gramophone, Terry Graham invited Kate to dance, and Kate's small hand lay warmly in hers when Miss Graham led her in a slow dance. Kate's hand was as still as a frightened bird, its heartbeat pulsed faintly in Terry's hand, which seemed to Kate to transmit a faint message, a small pressure that made her cheeks burn while her hand remained carefully neutral. She shivered when the buttons on Miss Graham's jacket touched her breast. They fell in love with the careful, but heedless love that thrives on the high-power diet that was a staple of boarding schools like Kate's and Marj's more than a half-century ago. Each school had a stirring motto: *Sursum Corda* for St. Anne's, *Vérité sans Peur* for St. Sophia's— "Lift up your Heart!" and "Truth without Fear." Marj loved St. Sophia's motto, but in practice she had found that difficult truths were always fearful. Both schools were under the wing of churches, both headed by high-minded single women. Honour and high seriousness were essential, sex was almost sublimated in a passion for learning, and great teachers tended the gemlike flame. Miss Graham, who had partaken of the body and blood of drama and poetry, shared them with her most gifted students. At a day-long picnic, she and her students read Euripides and Eugene O'Neill, were fired by the turbulent passions of Greek heroines and heroes, of the royal siblings: Iphigenia and Electra and their brother Orestes. "Iphigenia in Aulis," Kate is saying. "How somebody's grandfather did um-ah and..." she puts her left hand on her head and makes a sweeping gesture with her right. "Somebody's grandfather set in motion all that anger of the gods. Iphigenia has it coming to her because of that." She laughs hard. "Somebody was always getting it," she says. At St. Anne's, literature was as real as life. It possessed Kate, its words shaped her lips under the direction of Terry Graham. With her hands cupping Kate's ribcage, Terry felt Kate's lungs deflate as she exhaled, and then expand again with the intake of a mighty breath.

Miss Graham taught intercostal diaphragmatic breathing by which the breath is supported on a column of air drawn upwards to the bellows of the lungs. Kate was Terry Graham's chef d'oeuvre—the perfect instrument for voice. She shaped each of Kate's words, trimmed its blunt edges until it had the fine perfection of a flint arrowhead. "Don't say 'wes' win'," said Terry. "It's 'west wind.'" She was directing her class in a production of Shaw's *Saint Joan* and chose Kate for the role of Dunois, Joan's great friend, "a good-natured and capable man," says Shaw. "He is well-built, carrying his armor easily." Dunois, his page, and Joan are waiting for the wind to change so that they can cross the river Loire to join Joan's army. "West wind, wanton wind, wilful wind, womanish wind, false wind from over the water, will you never blow again?" Kate as Dunois (a bit of a misogynist) invokes the wind—with due emphasis on the repeated d's. What a glorious scene, Marj thinks, imagining the two schoolgirls, Kate as Dunois and Peggy Pennington as Joan. Kate longed to play the part of Joan, she tells Marj, but Miss Graham gave it to Penny Pennington.

Kate felt that she *was* Joan, the boy-girl. "I do not want to be thought of as a woman," Joan tells Dunois. "I will not dress as a woman. I do not care for the things women care for." She will never take a husband, she says. Marj hears a sextet of voices, the voices of Shaw, Joan and Dunois, Kate and Peggy, and Terry Graham, who cries out with real pain, "Not 'wes' win'!" Terry holds in her mind the solemn exactness of Dunois's joy, of Joan's, when the wind changes; tears will fill her own eyes when Joan, swept up in the grandeur and terror of her destiny, bursts into tears, flings her arms around Dunois and kisses him on both cheeks. "Dunois, dear comrade-in-arms," Peggy-Joan says to Kate-Dunois, "Help me. My eyes are blinded by tears. Set my foot on the ladder and say, 'Up, Joan!'" "Never mind the tears," says Kate-Dunois. "Make for the flash of the guns." "Ah!" cries Joan. Ah!—the expletive that propels Joan; Terry Graham explains to Peggy how that "ah!" can suggest eagerness, faith and victory all at once.

Marj bends her head over the table to inhale the fragrance of the frangipani blossoms that Kate has floated in a shallow bowl. Their petals have the matte texture of heavy silk, make an S-curve deep into the pale-yellow funnel from which sprouts a perfume-laden stamen. "What kind of a body did she have?" Marj asks. "You're waiting for the big drama, aren't you?" says Kate. Marj laughs. Kate will jump over the big drama, will lead Marj along false trails, then double back. She has made an art, Marj tells her, of not getting to the point. She will talk about the war, herself in the army. "And mind you, I was fat," she will say, "from all that bread we had at school."

"It was stiff rather than flowing," Kate says suddenly. "She walked stiffly and rather jerkily. Nice legs. And hands," she adds, "broad hands with long fingers and strong wrists. I was aware of her hands when she danced with me." Kate has doubled back again. She is a schoolgirl dancing with Terry Graham, who is wearing a linen jacket with covered buttons. Kate is wearing her school uniform, a black tunic and black stockings, a yellow blazer with two pockets gleaming with the emblems of success. It will take another breakfast time for Kate to explain the choreography of these pockets, how they changed places, how they were taken off to be embroidered with another championship, tennis racquets or a volleyball, captain of this or that team, or of a dormitory.

"I held her hand in the movies," Kate is saying. "Hold on, we'll get things straight. I've left school forever! I'm drinking beer and smoking cigarettes and sitting in little dark coffeehouses. I was wearing summer dresses and lipstick, and letting my hair fall down, and mind you, I was overweight, too, so I'm holding my breath and pulling myself together and trying to look glamorous. Oh yes, we're together, we're touching up in Her Royal Highness's cinema. Marj imagines an underground tremor, the passion between Kate and Terry Graham, picking up strength in Kate's last school year, and during the week when Terry, discreetly aloof, coached Kate and another of her best students, for advanced degrees in teaching. Now Kate has jumped to the tryst she kept with Terry when Kate's northbound train made a midnight stop at the town near St. Anne's, when the two met and went to Her Highness's for the late show. "The emotions running fairly high," says Kate. "It was in the movie house underneath the big hat, an away-from-school hat. She, too, is carrying a hat, sort of here. Wait, I'll demonstrate." She gets a wide-brimmed hat with a blue ribbon around it and continues. She has moved to the chair next to Marj and has put the hat on Marj's lap. "My hand is moving over the silky feeling, the back of my hand stroking. It was a big Australian hat. Sometimes her hand is moving, because she likes it, you see."

The emotions ran high; Kate describes the scene after the movie, in Terry's bedroom. "And we were on the bed kissing and hugging and I'm bold enough to undo the buttons. Still the schoolgirl; she is my teacher so I'm being cautious. I'm undoing the buttons and running my hand over the sweet boobs." But a last-ditch decorum that operated between teachers and students stopped Terry Graham in the middle of this scene. There was no love-making, only Terry's farewell kiss at the train station. "It was where you step up to get on the train; she suddenly kissed me on the mouth." It was Kate's introduction to the role of tongues in kisses. "I was utterly astonished by the sudden openness of this kiss," says Kate. Marj remembers back to the horrid sensation of the first real kiss and how she squirmed away from Bob, a minister-to-be, when she felt his thrusting tongue in her mouth. Now she watches the scene between Kate and Terry at the station with the sensual complicity of experience. It was wartime; people made passionate farewells on station platforms. They didn't even notice that the woman in the white suit was kissing the smaller, plumper woman on the mouth, that the smaller woman looked as though she had been touched with the fire of the Holy Ghost.

"And after that?" Marj asks. "After that I was writing her passionate letters and she was answering coldly." "Weren't you in despair?" "Yes, I suppose you would call it my first bout of grief." First Terry's cool answers, and then silence. Terry made a prudent choice; to answer, she knew, was to prolong the pain. Marj imagines Kate in a lifeless desert where there is not a human soul to confide in, not a single person in the world, no one in her family nor among her friends to trust with her incendiary secret. Now, because they love each other, Kate is sharing her secrets with Marj; in the time which is seeping into the present she will wish she hadn't. "She married," she is saying, "though she often talked to me about the rewards of staying single. She said I had the makings of an artist, and that women artists who marry have a hard time of it."

Marj is daydreaming. She is sixteen; she is in Mrs. Hunt's garden. She feels the presence of Mrs. Hunt, who teaches wood-carving, behind her, and Marj's hands, one holding a mallet, the other a chisel, freeze in mid-air. Mrs. Hunt (Marj does not know her first name) is praising the horse Marj has carved out of oak—its long straight nose and flaring nostrils, the pride and fire in the curve of its neck. A year later, in Philadelphia, Marj climbs the stairs to Mrs. Hunt's apartment and knocks on the door. She hears a child wailing. Mrs. Hunt opens the door; her beautiful face looks impatient and weary. Why has Marj come?

Now in her daydream she equates Mrs. Hunt with Terry Graham. Each married, each gave up her creative life. The memory of Mrs. Hunt, possessed by forms, happy about

Marj's fiery horse, the thought of Terry Graham, possessed by the drama of words, and by an image of Kate—how her body moved, her mouth spoke, by the blue language of Kate's eyes—took Marj back to the time before sex was born in her, when love flourished in hushed brightness, a change of body chemistry into molecules of light. She fell in love then, just as she does now, with images rather than with bodies, as she had fallen in love, months before they met, with an image of Kate. She looks across the table at Kate, who is humming, "It was just one of those things—a trip to the moon on gossamer wings. Frankie sings it, I think. We'll take the ferret—one of her playful word-changes—to town," she says, "and pick up our tickets to the Reef. Shall we do that, darling? Yes? Eh? Will that suit Madame?" She has assumed the persona of Mabel, a ninety-year-old housekeeper, both servile and cunning, who can always be depended on to make Marj laugh. There will be plenty of time for more of the real in the days to come.

Now Kate fluffs up her silky white hair, carefully puts on a bit of lipstick and some earrings, a snow-white blouse, a narrow scarlet tie, knotted with quick-moving hands, pulls on navy blue slacks and a pair of small white moccasins ("I got them cheapo," she says). They go out into the sunshine of another Sydney day, walk on a blue carpet of jacaranda flowers, are guided by a haunting perfume past the frangipani tree, to its fallen white blossoms on the sidewalk, spreading over the street.

Chapter Three

In the imaginary love-time, four months before Kate and Marj met, Marj made a trip to Amsterdam for the Feminist Book Fair. There were five letters from Kate waiting for her at her hotel. She felt Kate's love warming her, pouring through her and spreading happiness out to the world, precipitating her into friendly embraces with other women, without any sense of disloyalty, for she was sure that her joy would make Kate joyful. The years dropped from her, she spilled out her story to anyone who would listen, she was happy in the company of her friends and with the Australian women, editors and writers whom she would later meet again in Australia. She felt that the lesbian nation was in full flower, soaring on sisterly love, and she was borne up by acclaim for the film, in which she had come out as a lesbian, in a sunny field, to a woman her own age, who beamed and said, "That's nice!" The film had been the reason for Kate's first letter to Marj; she had seen it with her two best friends and it had made them happy, too, she wrote. It was as if a voice had said, "There, the word has been spoken, and there's nothing so terrible about it, is there?"

Marj and her friends in the film enjoyed its success; they liked to be stopped in the street and treated like old friends. "I like to be made much of," Marj wrote to Kate before they met. After they met, Kate caught Marj in the act of liking to be made much of, when she smiled like a cat and made a little deprecatory grimace that seemed to mean, "Please go on."

In Amsterdam, speeding across a sunny square, Marj had a vision: a blue-eyed woman would walk toward her, stop just as Marj was flying by. They would look fixedly at each other, burst out laughing and embrace with spontaneous passion. "I thought I'd surprise you," Kate would say. In the scenario, Marj's rapture contained a whisper of doubt. "You are no longer free," said the doubting self. She imagined a silken bridle over her head, the reins guiding her this way and that, a little tug of the bit if she embraced a friend too fervently or if she took time away from her ecstatic new bond with Kate to have a long talk with another woman. When Marj played out the scene in her head, she felt for the first time the difference between the easy swearing of complete loyalty in letters and the reminder in reality that she had made pledges to Kate that she might not be able to keep. She remembered the letter to Kate in which she yielded up her "precious autonomy." It had come into full bloom in her old age when she was alone and had all the space she needed to set her schedules and revel in the intense perceptions that germinate in solitude. She yielded it up with the naïve certainty that Kate, in turn, had yielded up her own. Didn't their pre-meeting letters suggest a harmonious entente between autonomies?

"You won't fall in love with any of those beautiful women in Amsterdam, will you?" Kate said in one of the five letters waiting for Marj. No, thought Marj, but she would spread her happy tidings. "I'm in love! I'm in love with an Australian woman I've never met!" she cried to Giovanna and Susanne, who both looked puzzled. When she ran into Lakshmi and Sybil, she repeated her news. Lakshmi looked grave, even mournful; she explained next day that she was afraid that Marj, once she came down to earth, was going to suffer. "I want you to be happy," she said. She looked like the Lord of Compassionate Glances, a terra-cotta Bhodhisattva who had entranced Marj in the Art Institute of Chicago. She swore to Lakshmi that she had never been happier. "Then it's all right," said Lakshmi solemnly, and kissed Marj.

The sunny route between Marj's hotel and the great meeting hall was alive with friends. How beautiful they were; they seemed to soar into the air like springboks. They wrapped their arms around each other's necks and laughed with the intense joy that filled every speeding second. When Marj and Marianne spied each other, they embraced with amazing enthusiasm as though after years of separation. "Five letters from Kate!" Marj knew that Marianne would delight in this piece of news.

So what if there was a groundswell of dissatisfaction among the more conscientious lesbians. As usual, their presence had been muted by the organizers, who had to answer to the City Fathers and Mothers. Answer to the honour of occupying the extraordinary building where the Book Fair was held, the pride of Amsterdam, an art nouveau chef d'oeuvre built with exquisite craft, inlaid tiles, stained glass, wrought-iron locks and hinges and great oak doors. If Marj had held it to her ear like a gigantic conch shell she could have heard the distant roar of traders and brokers, all shouting at once, and the whisper of ticker tape spilling over the splendid hardwood floor. Instead, in this hallowed building, she heard poets and novelists, feminist theorists and fearless activists, many of them lesbians. Thanks to the love in her heart, Marj was unconcerned about the worries of the organizers. A letter of protest was circulated, however, and she, too, signed it. Yes, it was bad, very bad, she agreed, laughing in the refuge of her heart. She was seventy-four years old and was drunk on lesbian presence, their defiant courage, their beauty.

"You'll go by yourself, won't you?" Kate and Marj had not yet met. Kate was talking on the telephone to Marj in Canada—about Marj's trip to Melbourne soon after her arrival in Australia—to represent the film, to read from her book. Kate's question could be read either as an assertion or an opportunity for Marj to say, "Wouldn't you like to come, too? Do come." She was aware of the difficulty of giving her answer an equal weight of finality and regret. "I think I should go alone, but I'll miss you terribly," she said. It was not the first test before they met of her sensitivity to Kate's hopes, nor the first of her failures to pick up one of Kate's cues. There was a silence between them. Then Kate said, "It's better if you go alone. You'll have more fun." For Marj there was no getting around the fact that her choice had excluded Kate and that her equivocation was unconvincing. Should there be yes-buts in the springtime of their love? "You'll have more fun." Marj could certainly not say yes, but she knew that Kate even at that great distance could read the yes in her head—the unsaid yes which gave her the power either to make Marj squirm or to let her off the hook. This time she let her off the hook, but with the proof that Marj's sense of freedom might mean as much to her as Kate did. Kate had discovered Marj's fear that she would circumscribe this freedom—in Marj's tactful little pulling-away, in her silence.

For her part, Marj has noticed the faint mockery in Kate's voice that marks the distance she puts between herself and the lesbian world. She recalls the letter she wrote to Kate before they met: "What is your relationship to the lesbian world community?" she asked. This question stirred up a long, troubled and defensive answer, a resumé of Kate's life of acceptance and denial, her courage of not-caring when she lived with Sandy, her younger lover. Each was a brilliant teacher, each had her charisma and her following of admiring students. When Sandy left her for another woman, Kate's whole life fell apart. She gave up her teaching job, she shunned the givers of comfort and counsel and moved to the anonymity of Sydney. Her sickness of soul dragged on for years. She believed that to others she was the person she "seemed to be." To the world, she said about her life with Sandy, the two of them were "best friends"; to their colleagues they were "whatever else they chose to believe." She got away with "*half*-hiding," she said. She is still homesick for the self of those years, the one who was happy and confident and made much of, the one who successfully practised the art of "*half*-hiding." If those who accepted this ambiguous outward image learned that she was "not altogether what she seemed, they would be sad," she thought and still thinks, both for her and for themselves. She knew that they would be sad because she had read textbooks which stated that homosexuality was abnormal or was a communicable disease. She knew that this was the general view. If people didn't show symptoms of dislike or horror it was because they didn't know that she was "one of the unmentionables."

Kate's letter stirred up panic in Marj. What had she done? She wrote back that she had been "Taurus trampling in Virgo's garden"; she had been careless and pretentious about the "lesbian world community." Hadn't she herself "half-hidden" for so long that she was almost a senior citizen when she came out? Marj's letter was typical of her conscience-stricken about-faces when she felt sick with guilt. She had wakened Kate's fears, above all her fear that to love Marj would be fraught with danger to herself. She had wakened her own fear, too—that to love Kate would mean to go back to her old caution. Their irreconcilable differences loomed long before Kate showed her anxiety about the correct position of two pillows. Let us declare friendship but not passionate love, those two pillows would say to Kate.

This letter of Kate's arrived five months before she and Marj met. Marj saw it as a watershed. She resolved not to provoke any more storms in Kate, to take delicate note of her fears. She felt full of loving intentions and was not yet aware that her best intentions would never be good enough. With this letter an almost imperceptible tug-of-war began between herself and Kate, who now, in Australia, wants to show that Marj will have more fun with *her*, than with *them*. Why does Marj, who is so happy alone with Kate, backslide the minute she is surrounded by *them*, why does she show such obvious joy and solidarity? This is my family, she seems to say, this is my world. She is saying, "I love women." "You hate men," Kate will say at last in exasperation. "I feel sorry for men." She knows wives who have chewed up their husbands for breakfast and spat them out. Marj will laugh, but with a sinking heart. Would the implications of Kate's accusation split them apart? "I believe that women can teach men to be less violent," Kate will say.

It does not occur to Marj that her five days in Melbourne will pass slowly for Kate. Marj will be made much of; Kate will spend five days wondering what Marj is up to. "Don't fall in love with any of those women in Melbourne; just keep thinking about me," she said. "I'll keep thinking about my Kate," said Marj. She is surprised by her elation as she relaxes against the velvety blue back of her seat, and the plane to Melbourne climbs into the upper air.

In Melbourne, Marj shivers in the coolness of an early spring. The wind blowing up the coast from the Antarctic Ocean gusts between buildings and old houses painted in muted colours: grey, beige, the pale green of reindeer moss, with tall windows framed in black. Marj is walking to the Hotel Windsor with some of the women she met in Amsterdam. There has been a showing of the film, the heady pleasure of answering questions about it afterwards, with a spice of official approval in the person of the deputy of Canada's Department of External Affairs. Marj and Kate have already laughed at the coincidence of their story with External Affairs, a kindly deus ex machina, which now steers Marj and her friends to the imposing Hotel Windsor for a fairy-tale buffet lunch. Marj will keep the menu: she wants to savour again in imagination Moreton Bay Bugs, Roll Mops, Mud Crabs, King Prawns and the peerless Pavlova—a thin shell of snowy meringue enclosing lemon mousse, created for the ballerina when she danced in Melbourne. Marj sits at a big round table, mesmerized by the lunch and by the soft voices, the seriousness and discretion of the other women. She has noted a difference from Sydney, where the buildings are the colours of Renoir's bathers, where Kate and her friends, creatures of sunshine, brim with laughter. Marj can imagine Kate here repressing a mischievous temptation to do one of her comic turns, or to say, "Come on, darlings, laugh, sing, dance! Life isn't that serious." She will be tempted in the feminist bookstore in Sydney when Marj does a reading. The L-persons (as Kate calls them) are as serious as nuns, she will say; they need a little shaking up. They should be teased about their solemn attention to Marj's every word, and Marj, too, should be teased about her basking look. She will be supernaturally conscious of Kate, vividly alive, sitting on the floor across the room in a cluster of women, while Marj reads. Their eyes meet; Kate looks as though she is about to burst out laughing. "Do you have a lover?" one of the women asks Marj, who looks at Kate for a signal. "No," she answers, "but I have lots of friends I love." "I thought you wouldn't like to be named," she tells Kate on her return. "I would have liked it," Kate answers.

Eva, Marj's hostess in Melbourne, lives in a big house with a garden full of white flowers: lilac, bridal wreath, roses, calla lilies, daisies, nicotiana. An English blackbird (a landed immigrant), is singing its flutey, caressing lover's song. Eva, a therapist, looks at Marj with steady-gazing brown eyes. She has been talking about the stately saraband of her women friends, in which lesbian lovers cross and change partners and resume their dance. "Without jealousy? Without quarrels?" "All conflict can be resolved," Eva answers. "That's what Eva likes to think," one of Eva's ex-lovers tells Marj. The next day Marj is driven down the coast, close to the apple-jade ocean southeast of Melbourne. An exhalation of smoky fog lies between sea and sky. Waves, gently crisscrossing on the long incline of the beach, meet and merge in long skeins, greet, pass through each other, slide back over the mirror of wet sand.

"The sea whisper'd me," Whitman ends the poem that Kate read aloud to Marj; her musical voice was rich with sensual overtones. Kate, her friends and family, the women Marj met in Sydney and Melbourne, seemed whisper'd by the sea, sung by the high chiming of the bellbirds, the warble of magpies, the mellow bass notes of currawongs at dawn. Perhaps they longed to enter into aboriginal dreamtime in which human beings become animals, a state of reverent attention, of listening and silence. The spell of silent attention is very strong in Australia, where the creatures of myth are never far away.

Kate, too, standing on the beach at Green Island, all in white against the white sand, is part of nature. She is holding a white hat in her right hand like a frisbee, ready to sail over the transparent turquoise water where Marj sees the dark triangle of a skate, sculling rapidly toward deep water with the rapier of its tail. Kate is white, blue, absorbed in the burning sand, the hot blue gaze of the sky. Her face is pink under its crown of white hair. Marj takes a photograph of her, will study her look of sceptical inquiry, her head full of unknowable thoughts. Is there a shimmering of air around her, a heat-shimmer of unspoken anger? Is it because of the woman in Kuranda who asked for the time, is it because of Marj's unspoken wish to see her again?

In Kuranda, they were on their way to the Aboriginal theatre, Kate ahead, walking swiftly. Marj's attention was caught by a woman across the street, wearing a sleeveless red-flowered dress; she was looking at Marj and tapping her watch. She looked like Kate, with a crest of white hair and a handsome sun-browned face. Marj shouted the time, Kate turned to look at them and hurried on.

She was almost running, propelled by her passionate love for theatre, which concentrated her entire being in an act of attention to *this*, of inattention to everything but this. She could not be distracted, as Marj was, by the woman who asked for the time. The seats in the theatre sloped up at such a steep angle that the audience seemed perched over the stage. It was easy for them to believe that they were participating in the music of flutes, reso-nant music-sticks and didgeridoos, that the soft-spoken men who introduced themselves, who explained the meaning of the designs painted in white on their bodies, and of the instrument each one held—that these men were close in spirit, when in fact they were as remote as starlight, their thought beginning aeons ago, their music echoing the earth, animal and birdsong, rain forests and burning plains. The show was about what the audience would call nature. The men belonged to nature; the clan designs they wore on their bodies meant that each was indistinguishable from that animal, that bird, that life-giving stretch of water. In their bodies they lived giving and taking life, the alternation of opposites, storm and calm, rain and drought, life and death. Their spirits held thousands of precise meanings and signs for the language of their world, and they presented some of their vast knowledge to the audience in simple terms. We were moved to tears of joy, Marj thinks, because they made us aware of a mystery that will always be beyond our understanding. They live in the invisibly mapped order of the Dreamtime, a continent that white strangers dared to trespass but could not destroy.

In their show in Kuranda, the dancers danced the mystery of their distance from the audience in time and space. They assumed the bodies of cassowaries and wallabies through a mimetic ritual by which hunters became the hunted. They danced how knowledge is forged by danger, they danced their own death and resurrection. At the end of the show, the whole audience rose, and Kate jumped up shouting "Bravo! Bravo!" Her deep attention, the attention of her entire body had lived the marvel of Aboriginal theatre, the profound entering into the beings of animals and of birds, the music, the dreamtime. Outside the theatre, some of the men were standing, their broad bare feet on the hot pavement were like lily-pads lying on water. One of the musicians was in front of Marj and she touched his back painted in the white abstract language of his identity. He turned and, almost in tears she stammered her delight. "We like to hear that people like our show," he said in his soft voice.

The next day Marj saw the woman who had asked for the time. She was waiting in line at the bus station, dressed in a pleated white tennis dress and sneakers; she had the muscular calves of a sportswoman. But she seemed to avoid them and Kate put on a burst of speed or hung back whenever she saw her. Did they know each other? Was each a ghost from the other's past? Marj wanted to strike up a conversation, to ask the woman to come to their motel at drinkie-time. She was just ahead of Marj when their bus from Kuranda arrived in Cairns; she sped away, effortlessly striding in her silent tennis shoes. Her motel was next to the one where Kate and Marj were staying. Marj felt a wordless clash of wills between her own wish to talk to the woman, Kate's wish to avoid her. Perhaps it was all in Marj's imagination; she often made up dramas with insufficient evidence. But why was Kate so evasive when she brought up the subject? "I'd like to talk to her," Marj said, "she looks nice." Kate didn't answer. Marj welcomed the moments when she and Kate moved close together in joy over natural wonders: the hot turquoise of the Coral Sea meeting the forest-garbed mountains, the explosive red flowering of Royal Poinciana trees, the animals and birds, the clustered bats fanning themselves with their wings at the top of a tall gum tree.

But at the Reef there was a distance between them. It was too hot to embrace each other; at night they lay in their separate beds in a state of restless insomnia. Marj remembers a breakfast table conversation in Sydney in the time of pure joy. She and Kate were discussing the General Confession, a shared part of their church-going past. "I have not done those things which I ought not to have done," said Marj and this made them limp with laughter. Kate had got rid of all that guilt-baggage a long time ago, she said. But Marj's guilt-baggage pursued them on the trips. What has she done now that she ought not to have done? What has she not done that she ought not to have done? She is standing on the balcony of their motel room. It is twilight; the day's heat still hangs over Cairns. A pink strip of sky is weighed down by heavy purple clouds, heat-lightning zigzags across them, without even a distant murmur of thunder or the staccato of raindrops. A Torresian Imperial pigeon stirs restlessly among the dark leaves of a tree near the motel. Its throaty coo sounds; the intermittent flash of its white breast in the shadow of the leaves is sending an indecipherable signal. Kate is in the stifling kitchen cooking their dinner, and a smell of fried fish wafts to the balcony. It seems to carry the vibrations of Kate's anger which Marj has already sensed without knowing its exact source. She has been reading warning omens into Kate's silences, and her inner trembling has begun, a fear like a dog's fear long before a thunderstorm breaks.

Chapter Four

The time: early morning in mid-December. The sky and harbour, the leaves on the trees, the pavements and streets, have been scoured by last night's thunderstorm, which turned the harbour lead-grey under a purple sky, drove the motorboats to safety, and the sailboats racing under their jibs before the east wind. Marj is wakened by the brightness in her room, she sees strips of sunshine dancing on the wall, and hears the sound of Kate's steady breathing across the hall. She and Kate separated coolly last night without even embracing. Their overheated discussion was interrupted by a crash of thunder and a gust of cold air that blew pages of newspaper off the coffee table. They ran around, closed doors and windows, and resumed the discussion: what is the ideal form of government?—Kate still angry because Marj had thrown it off course. Marj seemed not to know the rules for logical discourse; she particularized instead of starting out on the highway of the general. She proposed Sweden as an example of good government. Kate said that they were not talking about particular governments. Marj said, "Why not? That's the way I think, from the particular to the general." Kate said that she must think from the general to the particular. She looked at Marj with alarming severity; she had begun to shout. Unease now travelled the length of Marj's body. She said, "I can't talk about politics; I'm no good at thinking about politics." Her mind was full of lifeless dust; love congealed in her veins. This is our first quarrel, she thought; there will be others. They will begin during dinner when Kate's thoughts crackle, her voice roars like a bush-fire, out of the open kitchen window and across the courtyard. After the thunderstorm Kate's mind was still blazing, she intended to arrive by logical means at the ideal government. She had hardly begun her strategic moves and Marj already showed signs of impatience. "I think I'd like to go to bed," said Marj. Kate looked at her in disbelief. Hadn't they been engaged in a rational discussion? Hadn't Marj cut it off? And why? Because it made her uncomfortable. Marj said, "I don't see why you have to shout at me and make me miserable." Kate said, "I'm not shouting and I'm not making you miserable. I am trying to conduct a logical discussion." Marj said, "Damn logic. I hate it!" Many months later Kate will write in a letter, "You said, 'Damn your logic!' I was shocked by your display of temper." When Marj went off to bed, Kate's mind seethed with a sense of the injustice done to her whole way of being. Tomorrow she would explain to Marj that she had been trying to suppress one of the most important elements of her (Kate's) character— her passion for reason and logic, for getting to the heart of things. Hadn't Mr. Pond, reading the bumps of Kate's six-year-old head, seen her "insatiable desire to know the 'why and wherefore' of things?" "Logical, far-seeing," he had said sixty-two years ago, "She reasons equally well by the inductive and deductive methods."

The next morning Marj walks silently past Kate's open door to the kitchen and fixes herself a bowl of cereal, prunes and half a banana, sits down at the dining room table to eat it, is startled by the sudden appearance of Kate, the frostiness in her eyes, her quick glance at the breakfast table. "I was hungry," says Marj. "Hungry, were you, darling? That's cool." Marj has broken love's inflexible laws more than once in her life. Now she has done it again, for Kate sets store by the right observance of ritual. Marj has forgotten not to get dressed; she is not wearing Kate's blue velvet dressing-gown. For the sake of peace, Kate will overlook it this time, and since Marj seems determined not to mention it, she will not insist on Marj's reason for walking out on their discussion last night. Marj is grateful to Kate for not mentioning it; she thinks that this is Kate's acknowledgement that she musn't pin Marj in a corner that way. She doesn't understand that she has refused to accept Kate as she is, that she is denying Kate's passion for the truth. At another time Kate will explain to Marj that one or two other women in her life have been unequal to the sensitive acceptance of the whole person that love requires. They became friends, not *close* friends, she will emphasize. This time, the centre of their love holds, Kate's voice becomes suddenly gentle, and love rushes back into Marj's heart. The stubborn fog that made each invisible to the other has burnt off and they look at each other with glad recognition. But the wound to Kate's ego remains, and Marj knows that the two people who look at each other so lovingly now can no longer guess each other's thoughts. Their words, their gestures, will be perceived by each in new ways, they will punish themselves with misinterpretations. Kate: She has not measured up. She has disappointed me. I must try to make her understand what I am. Marj: I'm no longer safe. I must be careful not to make Kate angry.

"You will defuse any possibility of anger," Marj wrote to Kate before they met. She remembers the time when their voices caressed each other on the telephone and the smallest changes of tone were momentous. She remembers Kate's silence after her own pronouncement—"I don't want to live in England," then Kate's jump to attention, her single word, "*Sweet*heart?" which held the question, "What has happened to make you sound so distant?" The questioning alarm in that one word flooded Marj with relief; they had tested the bond that held them together, and the threat, like a heavy hand that twisted them apart, withdrew. It could never be more serious than this, Marj thought, for each instantly understood the whys of every possible difference between them and how to exorcise them. But, Marj now thinks, were the two emphatic syllables of that "*sweet*heart" more like a pennant hoisted, a warning in the calm before the storm? "How delicately, how intuitively we discovered each other. How *truly*," Marj will write, post-Australia. She will speak of the "transparency of trust" between them before they met, when, in imagination, they embraced in a garden of Eden.

"We slipped into each other's lives as though we had been there before," Kate will write. She speaks of "the mutual confidence that we were what we seemed." They felt comfortable in their resemblances, too comfortable to note that the resemblances contained differences like trip-wires cunningly laid and hidden. Marj, sobered briefly by Kate's fierceness during the logic-session, hopes that the ideal government will never again be the subject of one of their "hiccups"—Kate's term. Now Marj has resumed her giddy carelessness and skips along, saying anything that comes into her head. She likes to believe what was forecast in their letters, that they would be able to talk without restrictions or taboos. It is lunchtime on a sunny day; they are eating lettuce and tomato and bacon sandwiches on whole wheat toast. Kate has been calm and tender in their conversation about Emily Dickinson. "To see Truth slant," she murmurs. "I like that." To see truth slant—the way a painter looks at her subject, screw-ing up her eyes, or in a mirror, to see the subject as colour rather than form? Or she turns the canvas upside down; that way she will not be distracted by literal forms, she will not look at details at the expense of the whole? Then she sees what is missing, the bit of colour that brings light into the whole composition. Marj remembers reading a study of Dickinson's passionate poetry and letters to women. "Some people claim Dickinson as a lesbian," she says. *At last* had been her own reaction. After all the sterile arguments, after the heterosexual insistence and the studious denials, the blanks of censorship. "Where is your proof?" asks Kate; her eyes fix Marj with a cold glare. "I want you to tell me where you got that information." "I read it somewhere," says Marj. *"Where?"* Kate has discovered a perfect example of Marj's sloppy statements, made of flimsy evidence. Love will not soften Kate's outrage; her whole life as a teacher is at stake, her insistence on the avoidance of stereotypes, her determination to teach students how to think straight.

"Does it matter to you whether she was a lesbian or not?" Now Marj is slipping away from the point, Kate says angrily; she is implying that Kate is angry because it matters to her whether the poet was a lesbian or not. Marj has grasped at this straw, that the word "lesbian" contains a charge of dynamite.

She remembers her dream of the two books: *Truth* and *Real;* she and Kate would agree about what was true, what was real. But Kate's truth does not admit circumstantial evidence or interpretations that leap from the poetry. She wants a plain answer to a plain question: was Emily Dickinson a lesbian or *was she not?* Would Kate deny that Emily fell passionately in love with her brother's wife? A passionate friendship, Kate would say. Without sex. That holy of holies, which belongs to men, should not be touched by a woman. It is forbidden even to think that Emily Dickinson had a clitoris. Better to teach innocent young people that Emily Dickinson poured all her sexual energy into imagery. "Wild nights! Wild nights! / Were I with thee, / Wild nights should be / Our luxury!"

Marj wants to examine all the possibilities between yes and no, the terrain of desire. "Say, sea, / Take me!"—the body's monosyllabic language. No, they are going to address the question, the only question, says Kate's stern face. Next time I'll be careful, thinks Marj. She remembers from her past the first flashpoint in love's scenario, how she could be careful after one lesson learned, but the trip-wire would be laid in another place. She will tread on it, despite her knowledge that love makes lovers angry with the unreasonable, poisonous and punishing anger that flourishes in the love-state. Finally it can only be resolved in silence and with the merciful passage of time.

We are too old, Marj thinks, to be repeating the youthful patterns; there isn't enough time to undo our snarled differences, to remake our first trust. Pessimistic, as usual. Though in Australia she bounces back to joy with amazing elasticity. Kate, the optimist, thinks: we'll ride it out. Hiccups are inevitable. As for the hard-hitting exchange of views like tennis balls, Marj isn't up to it. She is like those others who could only accept the play-Kate, the clown, the role that Kate finds so easy. She knows that Marj is thinking, where is *my* Kate?

Marj hopes that she and Kate will never again have another logical discussion. Kate thinks that Marj has chopped off the discussion because she has a closed mind. To open a closed mind is a delicate and arduous task; Kate was rewarded many times in her past when a student, after long discussion, suddenly saw the light. From then on she could believe that he or she had an open mind, that is, one that was open to every new idea and challenge. She will be patient with Marj who obviously does not know the rules of logic. This time the question to be logically discussed is: why did Marj wait for seven months before answering Kate's first letter? Kate believes that logic will crack the mystery; Marj thinks that the answer lies in the illogical domain of memory, *her* memory. Doesn't she pile today's mail on yesterday's mail until a letter that has warmed her heart is suffocated and forgotten? But I can't say *forgotten*, she thinks, for perhaps Kate has been tormenting herself with the idea that her letter wasn't worth answering. "It was in a pile of letters," she says. "I get a lot of letters." "Not as wonderful as yours, of course," she adds. Will this give pain? Kate wants Marj to stop beating about the bush. In her saga of that first letter which she will relate to Marj's friends, Kate will say, "I said to myself, 'That's cool. Marj isn't going to answer my letter. So what?'" She likes the element of suspense in this part of the story, the fact that destiny was kept waiting. "During those seven months I might have fallen in love with someone else," she says to Marj. Marj says, "When I found your letter again, I reread it and thought, oh my god, I should have answered this long ago. It's a wonderful letter." Kate pounces, "You'd forgotten it." "I do often forget important things," says Marj. Evasive again. "If you forgot it, it couldn't have been all that wonderful, could it?"

Marj's evasive tactics are seen by Kate as a form of dishonesty; obviously, she cannot *take* logic. Marj thinks that Kate's exercises in logic create unnecessary differences between them, and her manoeuvres represent a refusal to be pinned down on a problem without a solution. Kate thinks that Marj is incapable of admitting that she is wrong; that's why she keeps throwing dust in Kate's eyes. Her mind is closed. Marj's closed mind is a threat to Kate's articles of faith, to her rational life, to her past life as a teacher. "The open mind genuinely wants to pursue the problem," she will write Marj, "even if the process and/or the conclusion is painful, involving A CHANGE OF MIND and beyond that A CHANGE OF BEHAVIOUR." Marj shows no signs of change, in spite of Kate's efforts, her patience, when she has had to "raise her voice" and repeat herself. She believes that the open mind can only be achieved by hard intellectual labour according to prescribed rules and that those who have succeeded at this task can never again have closed minds.

At the Great Barrier Reef on Green Island, Kate and Marj went to a Giant Clam hatchery where a stout man in shorts was, singlehandedly, attempting to save the species. An Australian friend of Marj's had told her of the miracle of seeing them years ago, upright on Reef beaches, six feet high. Since then thousands had been killed and eaten; their shells were made into birdbaths and baptismal fonts. The tourists gathered round a tank of sea water. The man in shorts showed them how the heavy shell began to close when the shadow of his hand passed over it. Its convoluted flesh, like a giant vulva, ringed with a thousand luminescent emerald green and cobalt blue eyes, began slowly to fold inward. Light-sensitive. Marj thinks, minds are like that, open or closed depending on the amount of light. The closed mind is opened by light, not necessarily the light of reason. She thinks that any mind can open or close; Kate thinks that minds must be trained to be open—once and for all. The openness has a logical vocabulary, she thinks.

Marj repudiates logic as a method for settling any problem in which the passions are engaged. There's no such thing as pure reason, she thinks. She remembers that Wittgenstein finally renounced logic as a method for answering all questions. He was dumbfounded when a fellow philosopher, making an aimless gesture, asked, "What is the logic of *this*?" Marj's dispute with Kate over logic fractured their harmony and sent a chill of fear through her body. They would never quarrel, they had promised, yet here was discord—between forms of discourse. She had wakened Kate's fierce pride as a teacher. And what had happened to their sense of humour, which they had sworn in writing never to lose? When it was most needed, it lay petrified in their hearts.

Chapter Five

Marj has come in the season between spring and summer, to thrilling birdsong and loud-crying colours: vermilion, deep red, purple, burnt orange and yellow, the quiet burning of pink sunlit houses, and the blue dance of the harbour. Marj's soul is full of soft-beating childish joy. This pure feeling goes back to her remotest past—at least seventy years ago, when she gazed at motes of dust rising and falling in a shaft of sunlight, or outdoors, looked up to find the source of a bird's song, and saw a song sparrow on the top of a telephone pole, saw its head tilted back and the feathers on its throat pulsing with music against the blue sky.

Kate enjoys showing her ideal landscape to Marj who has the sense not to gush; she keeps still, wonderstruck at every new epiphany. Kate has lived the Australian landscape all her life, it belongs to her almost as a spouse would in a long, happy marriage. Now it is doing its best to please Marj, as though it were determined to cooperate in Kate's grand plan for Marj's visit. Kate is wonderfully quick to see birds that Marj has missed; she puts out a restraining hand when she and Marj are trudging up the hill from the ferry dock after a day's outing. She whispers, "Kookaburras." They are perched on a powerline above Kate and Marj. The two kookaburras laugh like villains in a melodrama before flying off, and for a long time, the memory of that mocking laughter will have the power to bring Kate and Marj closer together.

The Australia that Marj sees with Kate and her friends is an Eden before the anger of the gods and the chaotic Babel of tongues. Within the calm white walls of Kate's apartment, a "hiccup" for Kate, a bad dream for Marj temporarily shatters the harmony that Marj lives and breathes. Before she and Kate met she believed that if their love was tested, they would look at each other and laugh. She had not anticipated Kate's lips pursed in cool scrutiny, or her suddenly wintry eyes. At the Reef, their glass-bottomed boat passed over stretches of sand and dead coral turned cement-grey; the rainbow inhabitants of the living reef had vanished. And then their boat skimmed over an underwater garden; jewelled fish slipped backwards under them in the current of the boat's passage, and Marj and Kate leaned close together. They met in places of assent where they agreed without the need of words.

Post-Australia, Marj will study photographs of Kate and herself. In some, they are out on Kate's balcony, bound to each other by the light meeting of their shoulders, a vibrating meeting of sleeves over warm flesh. In one photograph they are seated, leaning against a bronze sculpture of a dog; an electric current seems to pass between their thighs in trousers, between the bent knee of one and the leg of the other. Jacky is taking the photograph and shares in the complicity of happiness. Kate's friends love her, and by extension have welcomed Marj. Before Marj arrived they agreed that the transcontinental friendship between Marj and Kate was beautiful, though their hearts grew heavy at the thought that this stranger might take Kate away from them. Two months was a *very* long visit, wasn't it? But Kate reassured them with one of her inspired explanations. She said that Marj needed at least two months to get even a rudimentary impression of Australia. She said that she and Marj had many common interests, that it was amazing how they agreed about their favourite poets and composers, how much they both loved animals and birds. It was a challenge to Kate's planning-power to devise her itinerary, like a continuous banquet composed of Australian culture, exquisite food, and the grand panoply of nature. Kate was too afraid of hurting her friends' feelings to hint that her relationship with Marj had already gone over the top. That this was the reason for Marj to make the long trip and for Kate to propose a two-month stay.

Marj relaxes without pangs of conscience into the hands of Kate, Jacky and Barbara who have made meticulous plans for the perfect visit. They have chosen restaurants on the harbour and in glorious parks, they have bought tickets to plays and to the ballet in the Opera House, which sails along the edge of the harbour like a great chambered nautilus. They have set aside days for picnics, trips to galleries and the Botanic Garden, and to their houses with breathtaking views, with resident magpies, galahs and kookaburras in their gardens. Kate's itineraries will take her and Marj to every point of the compass. Marj must see only beauty; she will be protected from any spectacle of pain. She will know only indirectly that each friend has suffered from her own and others' illnesses, griefs, the vagaries of husbands and children, that each has witnessed death. For the now of each marvellous outing, they leave their anxieties and their families behind and laugh as merrily as schoolgirls on vacation.

"I had a crush on you at St. Anne's," Barbara will say in the middle of their farewell lunch party. They will be sitting at a table next to the open window of a restaurant poised over the waterfront—a Sydney scene beyond: sailboats scudding over the dazzling water, a cloudless sky and a breeze blowing in on them, ruffling a corner of the tablecloth. Barbara's grey eyes, as candid as a child's, will be fixed on Kate's face. In her memory she is tucked in her dormitory bed, while Kate, who is Captain of the dormitory, stands at the door. She is wearing her school blazer with a resplendent pocket over each breast. One of the pockets is embroidered with tennis racquets, baseball bats, lacrosse sticks, symbols of team successes, the other one with the school shield and motto, *Sursum Corda!* Barbara is willing Kate's blue eyes to answer her steady gaze. But Kate knows the peril of direct looks, knows already how to deflect them by not looking back. In the restaurant she will give a little laugh and say, "Oh, did you?" She says it impersonally, from her long habit of carefulness. Marj wants to pursue the subject of crushes, so critical in her own life at boarding school, where crushes were expected, permitted, were part of the fabric of school life. Not sex, of course; authoritative members of both sexes had decreed that any intimate touching between women was a punishable offence. At the restaurant, the friends will not pursue the subject of crushes. But a sweet sensuality will pass between friend and friend in this time, just before Marj goes back to Canada. A time when Kate's friends will become Marj's friends and Kate's life will still be running in Marj's veins.

Within Kate's domestic kingdom, Marj, who has begged Kate to let her help, sets the table and dries the dishes with a solemn sense of purpose and responsibility. In retrospect, she is aware of resemblances between Kate and her own mother, who had a trim, comfortable body like Kate's, without jutting bones, who, in her happy moods had the same sunny gaiety and lightness of being as Kate. In Australia, Marj does not think it strange that she feels so at home with her mother's body in Kate when she had been ill at ease with her own mother. There are infantile memories in her that acknowledge her mother's first passion of tenderness, and now Marj welcomes this in Kate's body and in her motherly authority. Marj's child-self longs to be perceived as good, as having done small tasks well. She feels the happiness of being allowed to take out the garbage, which requires a greater exercise of judgement than drying the dishes. If other tenants' garbage cans are lined up on the street, she will take her plastic bag to a shed at the back of the courtyard, open the latched door and seek Kate's solitary blue garbage can in the darkness. She will then put the plastic bag into it and carry it out to the street. She has a strong sense of Kate out on her balcony and of her eyes which follow Marj's itinerary until she arrives safely at the downstairs door.

Eventually, Kate will trust Marj to leave the courtyard, turn left, go up the street past the frangipani tree to a grocery store where she will ask for two lemons and a head of lettuce. Another customer is there; he is saying, "My mother-in-law is the whingingest person on the face of the earth." "Whingingest," i.e. the worst grouser, griper, sob sister. Combined with Marj's childish delight in any task Kate gives her, is the fear, a ghost of her remote past, that she will do something wrong. Sometimes Kate gives her the grocery list ("Pears Apples Coral Lettuce Mushrooms Shallots Mung beans Lemons Bananas"), a source of loitering and anxiety while she searches for the perfect pear or is hypnotized by an array of exotic vegetables. Sometimes she waits out in the parking lot in the sunwarmed car, where she thinks, she will tell Kate, of her perfectionism and of her "fossicking among the veggies." She will recount to Kate the marvels she has seen: a mynah bird singing on top of a ventilator, or a Blue Heeler, a bluish-grey, white-spotted herding dog descended from dingoes, that has been trained not to kill.

The breakfast times full of laughter continue. Kate is as likely as not to jump from the anger of the gods to the diphthongs that characterize Australian speech: "pie-ee" instead of "peh-ee," she says, "aw-ee" for "I," instead of "eye-ee." "Heh-oo neh-oo, breh-oon keh-oo," instead of "ha-oo na-oo," Kate says. "How now, brown cow, why do you frown down upon the ground?" "You speak very Anglo-American," she says, "the r-sound—a soft way of speaking American."

Kate takes off from diphthongs and touches down at the passionate solemnity of drama: Terry Graham's dramatization of *The Hound of Heaven* and her own of *The Ancient Mariner*. Two grand poems of guilt and redemption. The ancient mariner is burdened by the dead albatross around his neck (he has killed it) and the narrator of *The Hound of Heaven* is dogged by Jesus Christ in the form of a divine hound. Even if Kate claims to have got rid of her "guilt-baggage," Marj sees its shadow over her life, crisscrossing like the shadows cast by the spotlight that Kate set up for *The Ancient Mariner* behind a big cross, to suggest the three crosses of the crucifixion. She plays her tape of the performance, spoken by a seventeen-year-old boy whose voice had been perfectly trained by Kate, a mournful, intense voice that carried the drama of the long poem and its vision of storm and fire, and a hell of absolute calm. Kate chose the music: Holtz, Vivaldi, Mahler, that divided the narrative into sections, like a mighty oratorio. Evidence for Kate's brilliant gift for direction, Marj thinks, is contained in this fifty-year-old tape with an uncertain soundtrack. It was a link in the chain of disappointments in Kate's life story when a big success could be nipped in the bud by a director's move to another city or another continent, and occasionally by Kate's professional pride, and her refusal to compromise.

Marj and Kate have both been baptized into the language, the theology, the moral beliefs of the Fathers.

They have both become non-believers, but Kate ceased to believe without making Marj's journey from disbelief to lingering irreverence. Kate does not like Marj's impertinent responses to serious things; she respects the believer's belief. She does not laugh when Marj recalls her memories of the communion service and their visual sharpness: the upturned soles of shoes of all sizes at the communion rail, the sticking out of tongues to receive the Host, the self-conscious return of communicants to their pews, the faint smell of wine and the cardboard taste of the wafers. The continuous bubbling of laughter in Marj at breakfast time contains disrespect for the sacred; Kate still feels reverence when she recalls her father's communion service.

Kate has turned into her actress-friend, Lenny, a small woman like an adorable child. Lenny's hair is cut straight all around, as if a silver pudding bowl had been set upon her head; she wears a floating white dress as light as thistledown, and patent leather Mary Jane pumps. "Australia's sons, let us rejoice!" Kate as Lenny declaims the national anthem in a flat voice. She interrupts herself to tell Marj that in deference to the women's movement "Australia's sons" has been changed to "Australians all." "I love a *sunburnt* country" (she goes on), "I love her far horizon" (she shades her right eye with her hand), "I love her jewelled sea / Her beauty and her terror / The wide brown land for me!" (with mock fervour), followed by the electrifying "Core of my heart, my country!" She slaps her hand on her heart so violently that she almost falls over backward. "She pays us back *three*fold"—with an up-you thrusting of three fingers....

Now Kate is singing from *The Boyfriend*, lines which seem to have been written for herself and Marj. "It's never too late to have a fling," she sings. "It's never too late to fall in love." "The modern artists of today / May paint their pictures faster / But when it comes to skill I say /

You can't beat an old master!" Before they met, Marj had correctly imagined this fabulous Kate, the full-fledged comedian, singer and dancer, a fount of joyful energy. Perhaps Marj is too attached to Kate's appearances? She will try months later to chart the changes in Kate from open to secret; she will realize that in the time when her own critical sense was asleep, when (except for logic-sessions) she saw Kate as perfect in every respect, Kate was watching, taking note, and her work of analysis and reaction, of the noting of difference, was fully awake. It was as though Marj were trying out for a part, the role of Kate's committed partner, and little by little she was getting bad marks, particularly in the domain of pleasure. When they begin the harrowing of the past, Kate will tell Marj that she has never before lived with a puritan, some-one who measures out her drink in drops, who has a spare, slow-moving body, who has never had excesses of any kind. Kate will say that she had thought from her reading of Marj's books that Marj had discerned the tight-assed person in herself and was now more open to life. Eventually Marj will understand that in Australia her self is competing with two other Marjes—the writer of her books (apparently aware of her faults) and the woman in the film, who seems kind and generous-hearted. Kate begins in Australia to collect evidence of a flesh and blood Marj who is very different from her two alter egos. Marj is unwittingly building a case for herself as her opposite.

During the bad dreams, Marj feels the tightening in herself of an intractable NO. After a logic-session she lies restlessly in bed; her head seems full of the inert grey insulation material that was blown between the roof and ceiling of her house in Canada. She falls asleep and dreams that she is in an empty room with a child (the child-Kate Marj has seen in a photograph), who is wearing a dress with a round neck and short sleeves. In the photo-graph Kate's light-coloured eyes are looking straight at the photographer with a hint of challenge in them. It was the time when she was living the family nightmare; she had learned discretion prematurely. In her dream, Marj walks away from the child who follows and confronts her. The child says defiantly, "I may be sick but I can still talk!"

Marj thinks (in the Now of three years later)—perhaps it is hindsight that enlarges and sharpens these trompe l'oeil portraits in her head of Kate, the drastic changes of Kate's face from tender joy as alive as a summer wind, to icy winter, or—lively in a frightening way, a fire out of control. She remembers a scene in which she lived one of Kate's changes from remoteness to presence. She is ironing in Kate's living room; the ironing board is set up between herself and Kate who is sitting in the big blue easy chair mending a sock. The windowshade behind her is pulled down, backlit by strong sunshine that bathes Kate in a diffuse light. Kate's pale-rimmed glasses rest on the high curve of her nose. She and Marj look at each other in an instant of impartiality, when the compass needle fixes the true north and its quivering is almost stilled. Marj makes her way around the ironing board and sits on the footstool in front of Kate. She will remember how Kate held her needle suspended, how she licked the end of the thread and thrust it carefully through the needle's eye while Marj tightened the pressure of her knees in a vise that gripped Kate's legs. How Kate in slow motion fastened the needle into the sock she was mending, and lowered her hands, so that they gently cupped Marj's bent head, how softly, how rhythmically Kate's two thumbs stroked Marj's head, in a repetitive, passionless, absent-minded gesture of motherly comfort.

The morning after a logic-session (subject: why did Marj take seven months to answer Kate's first letter?), Kate has a questioning look in her eyes which Marj misreads as, "Will you forgive me for shouting so angrily at you last night?" In fact, Kate will explain, she wants the answer to a question: "Why do you chop off something I enjoy so much—the rite of drinkie-time and the free exercise of my mind?" Hadn't Marj written to her, "You'll teach me how never to worry you, hurt you or make you lose patience with me"? Now Marj seems not to have noticed that she has hurt Kate by denying her needs—"a huge denial of my self," Kate will call it. The question: will Marj try to understand me? will take possession of her. It is a question which contains another: will Marj accept me? Marj needs time to see that the corollary of understanding is acceptance; in the meantime, she believes with her customary hubris that silence without reproaches is her best policy in the delicate aftermath of an unsuccessful logic-session. She believes that they understand each other with (as she had predicted) "a delicacy of perception each for each." She wrote to Kate of "a marvellous time of listening to you while you fill in all the spaces of my knowledge of you, flesh them out—the events, the chronology. And the women in between." This preview has evidently given Kate the hope that as she recounts her life to Marj, Marj will come to understand that she must view Kate in the context of her whole life, not just that fraction of it that Marj is acquainted with. And she will explain to Marj that the raising of her voice is a frustrated response to Marj's refusal to continue a logic-session, Marj's "huge denial." Surely they would be able to discuss all this, for hadn't they agreed before they met that there would be no forbidden territory in their relationship? Surely Marj is the open-minded person of her books, too kind to let Kate suffer. Kate has already begun to feel that there is forbidden territory between them. "It has to do," she will write Marj, back in Canada, "with my obsession with logic!" She will contrast Marj's conduct during a logic-session to Sandy's, which made their evenings so pleasurable: "*Rational* argument laced with humour, so unlike war."

There were visions of rational argument in Marj's pre-meeting scenario, laced with humour, too, but the reality of the logic-sessions was beyond the reach of her intuition, which had perceived Kate as both a wise and patient teacher and a tender clown. At some point Kate will suggest that this captivating self is a persona; Kate is acting her. People mistake her persona for her "real" self, who is soberly observing and would prefer to cut all the comedy and emerge in the passionately serious light of truth. Marj has chosen to love the Kate who is easy to love. Wittgenstein, too, cared passionately about the truth of logic. In the film Marj saw about him, he shouts at his little pupils and pulls the girls' pigtails. He flies into a rage when one of them whispers, "I don't understand." Marj's failure to understand what Kate is telling her will grow in Kate's heart, become unbearably heavy; she will call it "a huge denial of myself."

In the time being of morning, the sun's rays warm the cold fluid running in Marj's veins, sweep aside the dust in her head. A discussion will only do violence to the perfection of the day, she thinks, and to *her* Kate, who seems to be born again every morning as fresh as a daisy. Kate need only look at Marj with a mischievous smile of welcome and they fall into each other's arms. Marj admires these quick changes, now and then even in the evening, when Kate may suddenly reduce the volume of her voice to quiet melody, or with a flare of humour (Marj has said, "Shhh!"), Kate goes to the kitchen window, leans out and shouts, "Can you hear me, Mrs. Preston?" They both laugh. Perhaps they will make love, not quite with the rapture of their first lovemaking but with a welcome sense of renewal.

Post-Australia, Marj will describe their love in a letter to Kate as "a delicious exchange of sensuality—like radiant heat." "Not necessarily sexy," she adds. And Kate will answer, "You write so magically about our love. We can talk and laugh about sex—without either of us being more demanding than the other." This is the truth without the warped hindsight of a more future time. In the long periods of truce between logic-sessions, they live under the spell of their first dream of a meeting. Marj had called their pre-meeting "the dance of multiple veils, the veils of getting acquainted, of liking and respect and the meeting of our minds and the meeting of our charismatic seduc-tiveness!" Marj's pre-meeting sensuality rode on the wings of music; she wrote to Kate about the phrase in the Waldstein sonata which enters like the sound of a distant bell and builds to a mighty song of praise: their story set to music, she said. She wrote of "the slow movements written just for us," and the final trio in *Der Rosenkavalier*. In Montreal before they met, she turned up the volume of the radio and stretched the telephone toward Kate just at the moment when the trio began. It was one of their coincidences that it began in the middle of a trans-continental conversation. "Can you hear it?" Marj felt faint with bliss. Music is part of their common language: "mine for you and yours for me," she wrote Kate, "as though you were touching my strings with a bow."

Post-Australia, Kate will try to make logic less intimidat-ing by reminding Marj of its role in the perfect planning of Marj's visit. "You think I'm efficient?" she writes. "Well if I am, it's because the mechanics of living comfortably (both physically and psychologically) seem to me to be easy little exercises in logic! I don't think of logic and imagina-tion as mutually exclusive. It's the *male* world that likes to separate these things." Marj agrees that this is an exemplary use of logic, perhaps the best use that can be made of it, since plans are apt to be more cooperative material to work with than human beings. In this context, logic is a form of art, Marj thinks, grateful to Kate for the patterns of splendid beauty that lie over the surface of every day.

The Kate Marj loves is at the heart of all this logical beauty, her tender Kate, foreseen in imagination, who shows up in dozens of photographs. The laughing Kate who, in the Blue Mountains, leans against Marj in front of the alertly standing bronze dog. Together they inhale and exhale the blue breath of the gum trees; together they gaze over a rolling ocean of treetops flowering a muted burnt sienna, and watch the white braided rope of a faraway waterfall measuring without apparent movement the distance from the clifftop to the forest floor. Kate and Marj are tourists, trespassers, no matter how reverent, on aboriginal land. They stand behind a pane of glass and watch the rainbow-coloured birds fly freely from their forest to a feeder inches away; at the Reef they see Prussian-blue butterflies fluttering in the warm air below a high gauze dome, and pandas in an enclosure, hugging sawed-off trees. Parrots and rosellas may also descend on picnic tables and nibble at the tourists' lunches. A man at the table next to Kate and Marj holds a crimson rosella upright and forces its beak against his sandwich; the jewelled bird beats its wings in panic. "You wanted to eat? Eat!" he says. Marj glares fiercely at him; his wife says, "Let it go." He lets it go.

For Kate and her friends the jewelled birds are familiars, Marj thinks, who come bearing tidings of joy and warnings of danger, of decline and extinction like the stretches of dead coral on the Reef. Marj feels the aching sorrow that epiphanies bring with them, more painful as she grows older, nostalgic regret for the time when song-birds returned on their appointed days every spring and Marj knew that it was April 12th when she heard an emphatic whistle followed by a lilting, restless song. The oriole was there in his heraldic colours, on the topmost grey branch of a still leafless locust tree.

Today, another radiant June day in January, Kate wrestles her little car out of its stall in the parking area and she and Marj go off with Jacky to have lunch with the poet who lives at the gateway to the harbour, on one of the great cliffs called the Heads. The poet's house is high up on the lee side of the cliff; the other side falls down to a red-brown rocky beach beaten by waves that have rolled westward for thousands of miles. Her house is perched on long steel legs and its back fits snugly against the cliff. The front windows are at treetop level; there is a continuous coming and going on the branches of rainbow lorikeets, king parrots, galahs and magpies. The poet, Madeleine, has had a glassed-in lookout and meditation room built on the roof and Marj imagines her there, her knees drawn up in the tiny space, her head on her arms while light pours through her and the warmth suspends her in a visionary state between sleep and waking. A poem begins to form, in her language of crystalline plain-song. Today she has invited her three friends: Kate, in her joyful, jesting persona, Alice, the painter, whose landscapes lie over a vermilion ground which throbs through them like the scarlet blood that burns in the faces of Renoir's children. And Jacky, with her kind brown eyes and warmly drawling voice; she is a listener who inhales life with her entire attention; Kate is at the centre of her universe. With the exception of Kate, the friends have married and borne children. Now they seem to say that nothing is more important than the wholeness of welcome. Each is an Australian microcosm, in each is the joy of being alive; they are welcoming Marj with the great bounty of Australian kindness.

The five women walk up the dry, sweet-smelling path behind the house to the top of the ridge, and the hot calm on the lee side suddenly changes to the buffeting of the ocean wind on their faces. They look down on the beach and the breaking waves and Marj thinks of the opposite winds on this side of the world, of the new night skies and the swarm of stars so dense that she and Kate have searched in vain for the Southern Cross.

The four friends in bathing suits are standing with their arms around each other just above the point at which the reaching waves edged by foam hiss backward. The women's sunburned bodies are braced against the friendly shove of the east wind. They laugh in unison at Marj who is taking the picture. Marj's jeans are rolled up, her white canvas hat is on her head. She, who used to lie in the sun for hours, is prudent now; she thinks of the two siblings who have been victims of the thinning ozone layer. She has never enjoyed being knocked down by a breaking wave, tumbled around and rolled helplessly over the sand and pebbles, choking on the salt water that filled her mouth and nose. Kate is one of several women in her life who worship the ocean and its stormy moods. Marj is more apt to be moved by a stretch of satiny water that merges with the sky and licks the shore with a whispering sound. "No rough strife," she wrote to Kate before they met, apropos of their future lovemaking. She thinks of one of Courbet's paintings; he is standing, a tiny figure in the vast seascape, on a rock that juts into the ocean. He is dressed in a dark, formal suit, he holds his hat aloft and salutes the glorious day and the tumbling waves at his feet. He celebrates, in this instance at least, without getting his feet wet. The title of the painting is *Bonjour, Monsieur Courbet!*

Chapter Six

On the day Marj goes back to Canada her heart is full of love for Kate, and her mind holds their triumphant story. She will tell her friends that the true story is even better than her scenario. She and Kate embrace at the airport with longing and regret; the time before Kate's trip to Canada—six months—will pass quickly, they tell each other. They embrace with seasoned passion, heedless of onlookers, and kiss their hands to each other just before Marj passes through Security.

Marj returns to frigid temperatures; her garden is buried in snow—smothered, like the dining room table under its burden of two months' mail. She has escaped all this in her never-never land with Kate; now her mind seems to wobble and go blank; she traverses a panic of forgetfulness. She was young in Australia; now she is irredeemably old, like the people with wrinkled faces who emerge from their youthful sojourn in Shangri-La. Her younger friends say reassuringly, "We forget, too." Marj has dreamt many times in her life about losing keys, glasses—symbols of understanding and vision. She translates snow in her dreams as the blank mind, the frozen memory of old age or death, the barrier at which memory is halted. This time, everything turns up after a few days. Marj writes to Kate, "The little iron bench near the back fence looks like an albino boa constrictor that has swallowed a wombat." Her mind and body have come to life again and she longs for Kate. "I stand against every inch of you," she writes, "and we love each other in our entirety. How lovely it is to know all this once and for all and forever." Kate answers, "Your love is (in my experience) UNIQUE."

Marj writes to Kate that she has begun work on *The Time Being*; she tells Kate "how much I'll need your help to make it precise. It will be made of 'scraps, orts, fragments.' I know that whatever I do Virginia Woolf will already have done it and that doesn't matter at all. She's our spirit guide and says, 'Whatever comes into your mind, try it.'" The words: "Try it" are Marj's wings. She will take off on her own, encouraged by Marianne, who after reading Marj's pages, says, "Kate will love it." "No, she won't love it," Marj says. She knows in one part of her mind that Kate will want to correct what she sees as grave errors of interpretation. This knowledge, in a minor key, accompanies Marj's frail hope that Kate will respond to her ode to their joy. When Kate comes to Canada, Marj will show her some tentative pages and Kate will meticulously correct place names, dates and the names of cats, as if that will help to correct the more serious error that Marj is making: her perception of Kate's willingness to be the heroine of their love story. Kate will not express her dislike in words, only with a look that Marj fears, remote, pale-eyed. Post-Canada, she will describe Marj's view of the book as "US for material." And Marj will think, hasn't the subject always been US and our time being? Unseen, unknown to each other, two time beings that met and merged in US? The book would be a meeting of the two books *Truth* and *Real* in Marj's dream; it would bring their pasts and presents together.

Marj begins to assemble her fragments from the great web of connections that made her meeting with Kate certain. She remembers a breakfast time when Kate read from MacNeice's *Columbus*. "But what you've never seen—that's what sticks in your mind," says Columbus on his way to landfall, while the Faith Chorus sings, "When we cross the Western Sea / All these things shall be, shall be." Hadn't Marj's vision of Kate stuck in her mind and propelled her across the Western Sea? It was amazing how everything seemed relevant to herself and Kate, *their* love, how eagerly she grasped at these identities in art, in landscape or from the unexpected vision of a bird with a message for them alone. It will be the same when Kate comes to Canada, Marj thinks. She writes to Kate out of her confidence in what they share. "Your thumb was moving between all my fingers and into my palm where I held it fast while the adagio made my heart beat because it's one of ours that we'll listen to when you come."

During the months that divide Kate and Marj, summer to winter and winter to summer, each is on her continent, each is in an opposite season. Marj writes, "The pendulum of us swings back and forth across the globe, my moon rises and yours sets and it's the same moon." Kate checks the weather in Montreal in the Sydney newspaper and says on the telephone, "It's minus 18° there and here it's 30°." They exchange thousands of words, with loving greetings, loving endings, like hands clasping, each tenderly clasping the other with her eloquent words. Marj's letters are happy; she is still living inside Kate's aura, her letters to Kate flow out in a river of high spirits. But almost from the beginning of their separation Kate, along with all her tenderness, despite her certainty that Marj's love for her is "wondrously STRONG," has felt what she calls a "niggling 'sort of' unease." It has to do, she says, with "forbidden territory," her belief that there was none between them, for hadn't they both sworn before they met that they would be able to talk freely about anything? But in Australia Kate discovered that there was forbidden territory, subjects at which Marj balked, which she refused to discuss, and, writes Kate, "it has to do with my obsession with logic!"

Kate launches herself into her defence of logic with the apparent certainty that she has only to clear up a little misunderstanding by Marj, that she need only explain the good uses of logic, "at the very heart of problem-solving," she says. Marj feels that logic has crept into the heart of their love like a life-threatening virus; she can feel its invasive presence, making trouble for them. For her, certainly, the slings and arrows of Kate's technique make her subjects forbidding, if not forbidden. In Canada, Marj scurries away from the subject of logic and writes, "I've started a beginning of my book. It's about blue eyes, a meditation on the power of *your* blue eyes."

Marj has become hard-nosed about her book, already aware of the hazards of submitting it to Kate's sense of what matters and what is correct. Below the cheerful melody of love Marj's self is reclaiming its perceived rights and taking back elements of its "precious autonomy." How happy it had made her to believe that she had yielded it up! But in Canada now, alone with the accumulating orts and scraps of her book, she remembers Kate's withdrawal in Australia as co-writer by way of a graceful abstention. At this high place of their love, Marj realized that her dream before they met of a shared book had been a mirage. Did she agree too soon to Kate's bowing-out? Mightn't it have been, once again, a test, like Kate's saying about Marj's invitation to Melbourne, "You'd better go by yourself. You'll have more fun"?

In the period between Australia and Canada, the melody of the story runs over chords in a minor key. "I love you my darling darlingmost adorée," Marj begins a letter and Kate replies, "My beautiful one, my darlingest heart." In the same letter Kate begins to use a yellow marking pencil to emphasize her points. "I don't think you have *quite* the same degree of TRUST in me?? You're more ready to respond as though I'm criticizing or pushing my point of view?" They have been writing each other about Kate's trip to Canada. Marj is never precise enough for Kate. The difference between their two planning techniques now crystallizes. In Australia Kate's genius for planning determined their schedule to the last detail; in Canada Marj's easy-going plans contain her faith that everything will turn out well because she and Kate love each other. Marj is an amateur, Kate is a professional at the business of organization. But, put to the test, Marj wants to surprise Kate with her efficiency. The yellow pencil is Kate's voice of frustration. Marj's loosely knit plans do not inspire Kate's trust; it is part of Kate's nature to nudge, to remind. Like the weaver bird she must patiently build with the end in sight, the perfect structure, created with a knowing sense of the basic twigs, followed by a judicious selection of pliant grasses, and finally the down from bursting seed-pods. Marj is wrong to think that she can build just as good a nest in her own way. There is only one way—that of the weaver bird. The strands holding Marj's nest together will pull loose and when Kate comes to Canada, the nest will tumble to the ground.

From the beginning of their separation Kate's letters have begun lovingly, her handwriting runs steadily, and Marj imagines her graceful ease, her knees rising and falling, her feet rhythmically touching the ground with exactly the same distance between each step. Kate writes with the knowledge, she says, that Marj loves her and wants to understand her "obsession," developed during her years of lecturing, directing plays, writing of all sorts—with "getting it right." Marj has noticed her states of preoccupation, hasn't she, when Kate withdraws into herself? Yes, Marj has noticed, can feel the vibrations of Kate's concentration in her preoccupied states, the silent music of Kate's being. Marj's unease springs from the sudden call to attention of the yellow marking pencil, which has swept through Kate's words: "Getting it ABSOLUTELY RIGHT within our relationship."

The yellow pencil repeats the message of a previous letter, and of Kate's fruitless attempts to explain herself to Marj in Australia. Logic is getting not just *it* right; it is getting Marj right. Perhaps Marj will yield to Kate's patient pressure, just as Kate's students used to yield, slowly, to let light into their minds, which opened like the great clam's shell. ABSOLUTELY RIGHT—the goal equal to Kate's patience: for her, perhaps, a joyful certainty; for Marj already a threat. She writes to Kate, "I think how precious our love for each other is, how we have to hold it in such a way that no harm can come to it; we musn't let things go wrong or something come between us, some tiny angle of error that widens." In Australia the angle of error began to widen in the first logic-session when Kate's voice rose. In Canada Marj remembers how love seemed then to drain from her heart, to be replaced by a cold liquid like embalming fluid.

In Canada Marj understands via Kate's letters that logic is the supporting strand for the grand structure of Kate's life—the warp, under and over which runs the woof of drinkies—that logic gives Kate the right to be passionate in argument, and that righteous excitability (the speech of the yellow pencil) is a bright strand in the woof. Kate as master builder has made it impossible to isolate a single strand without threatening the whole. Against the whole, Marj is powerless; it is both inflexible and resilient. Marj calls up her memory of the evening in Australia with Kate in futile pursuit of the ideal government. She was shouting at Marj, whose mind had gone blank. She paused, picked up the brandy bottle and tipped it with a steady hand over her glass. Marj looked at it with dislike; it was her enemy, a kind of Iago who would turn Kate against her.

To her own surprise she burst out, "You're fuzzing up your beautiful mind with brandy! You're in the process of ruining your life!" She could feel her face turning crimson, the blood was beating in her head. Kate stared at her. She said, "Do you want me to stop drinking? I will, I will." It was an instance of her reckless daring, a glove thrown down for Marj to pick up or not. But what would be the price? Marj thought in sudden panic. She hesitated. "Well, not stop *entirely*," she said. Stop before your anger begins, she meant, before I become the target for it. She did not say any of this. Kate had made one of her instant changes to calm lucidity and to her musical mezzo-soprano.

Back in Canada, Marj writes to Kate, "Each of us should be sensitive to signs of distress in the other." Not stop entirely, stop short of signs of distress. It occurs to her that Kate perhaps interprets her own anger as a sign of distress, and that danger lies in Kate's apparent decision to do something to please Marj that would insult her own soul, her sense of her self. Even to watch for signs of distress in Marj would cramp Kate's style and suggest, as she will tell Marj, that she "had to mind her P's and Q's." She will react angrily when she realizes that this was exactly what Marj hoped she would do; worse, that Marj thought of Kate's minding of her P's and Q's as a victory for each of them. Marj basked temporarily in Kate's undeclared peace at the very time that Kate was chafing at Marj's unwarranted interference in her whole existence.

Kate had discerned Marj's anxiety and refusal to go on in a logic-session, not as signs of distress, but as a challenge, an insult, an absence of trust, a pretext for her legitimate anger. During the time of their separation, Kate's letters to Marj put her whole self, of which drinkie-time is an essential part, on the line. Hasn't Marj noticed, Kate asks, that brandy is an important ingredient of her "much-appreciated social energy?" In her professional past, drinkie-time came as a reward after a hard workday, with "its companionable sitting-at-the-table and its exchange of ideas, intellectual fireworks and rational debate." Kate's defence of drinkies, during these months when their letters begin and end so lovingly, is part of her ongoing struggle to get things right. Marj writes from Canada that she "stopped sniping" in Australia about the connection between brandy and the intemperate decibels of logic. To Kate, Marj's talk of "signs of distress" is a renewal of sniping. She writes, "I *thought* (as time went by) that you could *see* that the brandy was *NOT* necessarily responsible for 'trouble'. I thought it had *genuinely* become an O.K. thing for me to have." A plea that touches Marj's heart without changing her mind. For Marj, not sniping in Australia was a fair exchange for Kate's restraint. For Kate, as she will make plain, the restraint which began as a gesture of goodwill becomes an intolerable infringement by Marj of Kate's rights.

Kate's letter, despite its excitable punctuation and emphatic yellow pencil, has been written in a spirit of negotiation. "I like to think," Kate writes, "that our differences might enrich us, rather than give pain." She says that in the process of discovering each other, "we have come a very long way already—so much so that it's a miracle." Marj imagines her sitting out on her balcony, writing her letter on the little round table, with a drinkie and a bowl of cheese snacks at hand. It is late afternoon, a cruise ship has given a deep bellow of farewell and is moving slowly out, green and yellow ferries are crisscrossing the harbour. The square-rigged schooner, *Bounty*, glides past with her sails neatly furled on the yards while laughing voices are borne to shore by a tranquil wind. Marj imagines Kate sitting with a drinkie in her hand as dusk comes on and the banners of coloured light fall over the water. She has put aside the yellow pencil and is breathing intercostal diaphragmatic words on paper: "And we'll go on loving each other," they tenderly exhale.

Marj writes: "Our love—a delicious exchange of sweet sensuality—like radiant heat, not necessarily sexy."

Kate writes: "It's one of our great great strengths that we can talk and laugh about sex...and be physically close without either of us being more demanding than the other. And we'll be talking and laughing *together* again soon." The yellow pencil has given emphasis to this prediction. So it can signify cheerful expectation, Marj thinks, as well as the stentorian, "Listen to me!" Perhaps her fear of it is exaggerated? Kate and Marj still love each other, midway into the months of their separation. Each believes in the other but is pleading the case now for her whole self; not only her lovable self of the time before they met, but also the hidden self that has begun to refuse compromise. In their first letters they found only subjects for agreement; in Australia, subjects for disagreement seemed suddenly to flare from underground and then subside. We are old, Marj thinks in Canada, and each has fashioned her way of life. In Australia, Marj was delighted to follow Kate's program, from the breakfast ritual through the day's marvels to the endearments of bedtime. In Canada, she returns to her own austere timetable. She does not consider the possibility that when Kate comes to visit, Marj's schedule may seem to Kate to be an absence of concern for her welfare.

Kate's handwriting runs steadily forward, she is intent on her goal—the moment when Marj will understand that her mind, closed to logic, is the impediment to the development of what Kate calls their "soulmateship." The male world, Kate writes, likes to separate logic and imagination, intellect and emotion. Men allow women to play with a few male qualities, she says, but keep for their own logic, analysis and objectivity. She suggests that women have a more creative, a less heavy-handed way of using logic to solve problems. Marj admires Kate's skill in pleading the cause of logic as if it were a bashful suitor. Kate's logic, Marj realizes, is feminist, is a form of art, a sublime game. It is the art that governs Kate's decisions, so interwoven with her life that to deny it, to mock it (and some people do, Kate says) is to deny her in her entirety.

Marj believes for a time that she and Kate are playing a game of trans-Pacific tennis. "We've had quite a lot of give and take," she tells Kate on the telephone. "You've gotten in some pretty good shots." Kate says, "Have I?" Marj has begun the conversation by telling Kate that she is going to get a letter exhorting her to creative effort. Creative effort is Marj's cure-all, the remedy for accidie, the faintness of soul. After proposing to Kate the intimacy of doing a book together she now has a vision of all the reasons why this would be impossible. They have different ways, she has realized, of getting it right. She wants to persuade Kate to write her own book—*Truth* or *Real*. Their two stories will twine and interlock like lovers, they will explore their lives in the spirit of the breakfast conversations when Kate was so candid and unafraid. Absolute rightness, Marj thinks, will happen when each concentrates on her own work. Though Evelyn, the sage friend who had correctly foreseen lovemaking between Kate and Marj, now warns Marj, "Don't push Kate about creative work, don't make critical comments. She's too vulnerable."

To Marj's surprise, Kate, apropos of creative effort, replies on the telephone, "That's all right, I need it." "You need it?" Marj says. "Well, if you don't like it, you can say, 'Piss off, shut up.' But if you mind," she adds, "I'll be sorry." "Don't be sorry," Kate says, "I'll say it to you, too. It's not your fault if I'm vulnerable. I have to do something about it." She has not taken offence, she has answered gently. It is as though, standing near calm water, she has picked up a skipping stone, wafer-thin, and with a strong movement of her wrist, has sent it out, lightly kissing the surface, and its overlapping circles reach all the way to Marj. "Between us there will be a transparency of trust," Marj wrote before they met.

Thousands of words are exchanged between them during the months that divide them, loving greetings, loving endings to their letters. "My love and lover, with whom I'm mated for life," Marj writes midway through the six months that separate them. She writes in her journal, "My best most attentive and loving half is with Kate and my incompetent, critical, discontented and weary half is on this continent." This is a load of codswallop, but she does not yet know it. Her words flow out in a river of hopes and certainties; they express her hope that words can tame the storm she can sense brewing in Kate. Yet she has anxious dreams. In one dream her car runs off the road into a pile of dry oak leaves; she looks and cannot find someone to help her out.

"How delicately, how intuitively we discovered each other, how *truly*," Marj writes, "for I know that our first perception was the truth and that the defensive stand each of us has taken is not the truth." She still has the fatal confidence of love, renewable, resilient. Kate tells Marj that they can discuss anything, as long as each has the other's welfare at heart. "Let a thousand flowers bloom," she seems to say. "So much ground we haven't covered," Kate says. She has conveyed so little of the total Kate, whereas Marj has already said everything there is to say about herself in her books. "What needs to be said," says Kate, "is huge in its substance." It is her substance, her shortcomings, too, she emphasizes, which she wants Marj to understand in a way that "increases rather than reduces" Marj's love. Is she talking about getting it absolutely right?

Marj goes to Florida for two winter weeks. "So much here is like Sydney," she writes in her journal, "the bougainvillaea, hibiscus, jasmine, big fig trees. The exquisite colour of the water yesterday—a milky aquamarine with a soft grey-mauve sky over it. Hard rain last night and palm branches slapping at the house, swishing like waves receding." She is spending two days in Marianne's little house in Key West, in the upstairs room crammed with the materials for Marianne's new novel, her orderly chaos. "Marianne is being lovely," Marj writes, "kind about my stupidity." Marj has rented a car and gets regularly lost. They have dinner with two warm-hearted friends: "We laughed and told our falling-in-love stories and drank a toast to Kate, and though I was half-dead from all my non-compos-mentis lapses all day long (en route from Montreal) I felt happy." They passed Marj's laughing photograph of Kate from one to the other—a close-up that Jacky had taken to show the blueness of Kate's eyes, and Marj bathed in reflected light from Kate's face, the beguiling tooth that punctuated her smile, and her seductive eyes.

At Sugarloaf Key, with her friends there, Marj feels the dissolving of all anxiety in her nervous system and the peace of understanding and being understood. It is a community, mostly lesbians, waxing and waning as women come through, activists in one way or another, artists, therapists, carpenters and builders; they show videos and talk about their lives. Sometimes they are rocked by differences, but they try to make them plain, talking them out even if it takes days. They are like archaeologists, who clean off earth-covered shards, grain by grain, with fine brushes, with feathers. Perhaps they will discover a piece of an ancient weapon, perhaps a mirror or a little clay lamp. In the same spirit, in dream-sessions they analyze each other's dreams.

In Marj's dreams she is being chased, is crying out for help; she dreams of fear, her dreams construct fables about herself and Kate. In a dream she sees, spread out on a beach, the loot from a sunken ship and a man who comes toward her, carrying the figurehead of a woman. The man is herself, she says in the dream-session; the figurehead is Kate, the woman on the ship's prow, who draws the ship along with her, the ship of her life. Marj is a false beacon, someone on the high land holding a lantern that will draw the ship to shore where it is wrecked. Kate's life, herself as figurehead, are jumbled on the beach—loot for Marj, from Kate's point of view. And Marj has the nerve to grab Kate herself and try to make off with the pieces of her. The dream is about the scraps, orts and fragments of Marj's book.

But the figurehead is also yourself, they say at the dream-session. The decided and pitiless you, as you sometimes see yourself, is carrying off the story of Kate, or your story of Kate, for you're equally the subject of the book. The ship contains the material for the book, its hidden cargo, now in the form of jumbled loot on the beach. The figurehead, before the shipwreck, broke the waves' violence.

At the send-off for Marj in Florida, her friends make a circle, their arms around each other's shoulders, and sing. "We sang (to the tune of 'Frère Jacques')," Marj writes to Kate, "(Wonderful old women, wonderful old women! Wow! Wow! Wow! (repeat) We can do just anything! We can do just anything! Wow! Wow! Wow!) And all laughed, of course." She returns to winter in Montreal, to temperatures below both zeroes and snow that almost spills over the fence in her garden.

A sick friend comes to stay with Kate. Kate takes her to the hospital for treatments. She assumes the caretaking persona of her mother, puts aside work on her novel; her letters become listless and imprecise. "Just lately," Marj writes, "you've spoken of yourself as 'an old potato,' ruefully, as though some kind of reasoning process has killed your faith in your creative self. You've been aware of growing old and of physical breakdowns in yourself, and I feel that you've gone through a crisis of doubt and depression, and finally, resignation—the rueful, 'I'm an old potato.'" Marj has found the Rune that Kate sent her before they met: "It is time to turn again and face the future reassured. The sharing is significant since it relates to the sun's power to foster life and illuminates all things with its light. I still believe," she goes on, "that our love has freed you to stop doubting your powers, to say anything you want. I feel that you're still grieving for the part of your life with Sandy that allowed you to feel fearless, in the context of your life together as two dynamic teachers and daring feminists. I'm aware of the confidence I haven't given you—of your disbelief in yourself—stopping work on something that started beautifully, your sense of growing old, the painful reminder of your wrists, as if to say, 'Look, my body agrees with my doubts.'"

A darkness between continents falls; Kate's letters are opaque, she has put aside the yellow pencil. Marj has moved to the country for the summer, with her cats, her dog and all the material for *The Time Being*.

On the telephone, Marj squeezes out of Kate, who has begun by saying, "I'm going away for a little trip," that she is having an operation. Nothing serious, says Kate. She tells Marj to get news from Barbara, only from Barbara. Barbara is the buffer, kind, reassuring, between Kate and Marj's anxiety. Barbara gives Marj the basic information: Kate got through the operation very well, "but it's all much longer than I thought. They're keeping her longer. It never occurred to me that it might be cancer—but it wasn't. She has a scar running halfway around her neck."

"My mixed feelings of joy and churlishness," Marj writes in her journal after her conversation with Barbara. "The churlishness is pure ego." But, as Kate's closest friend, her demons whisper, doesn't she have privileges? of worrying? of being possessive? No, says the reasonable self. She suspects that Kate fears that she will upset the structure, so carefully wrought, of her (Kate's) safety, guarded by Barbara and Jacky, that Kate fears the extra burden on her of Marj's anxiety and believes her own silences to be thoughtfulness for Marj.

Ten days after Kate's trip to the hospital, she calls. Her voice, her laugh are a little hoarse but beautifully reassuring, and all the subatomic particles of Marj's being are rearranged. Her mind, which has been in a pandemonium of fear, grows calm in the seconds when Kate murmurs, "I thought I'd let you know that I'm back. I didn't know, they didn't tell me, that it would be a big operation." "They didn't tell you!" What's left of Marj's no-confidence case against Kate, the merciless battering in her head, turns against the doctors, convinced that women become hysterical in the face of bad news (a serious operation, tubes, after slitting open the throat). The doctors are a worthy subject of outrage. Kate has had a go at them in the hospital, she says. "You pretended to me that it would be a minor operation. You just cut into me," she told them. "And I'm not done with the subject!"

"My *you* has returned," Marj writes to Kate. Kate is translucent again, she is receiving Marj's messages of love and transmitting her own. They write, "je t'adore" at the end of their letters; Marj says, "I love my Kate with feathery tenderness." On the telephone, "we talked as we had talked last year," says Marj—Marj, returned to life, imagines a scene of Kate in the hospital: "your gorgeous eyes blue-glinting at the nice nurse. I can hear her regaling her friends, 'My patient is some beautiful woman! You should see her eyes. And she laughs even though she looks like an echidna with all those bristling tubes. If you have a chance just go by her room and maybe she'll smile at you.' Nurse II: 'Watch it, sister, you know how susceptible you are. It seems she has a ferocious lover someplace in Canada.' Nurse I: 'Well, I better make the most of my time, then!'" Marj forgets that Kate would certainly not have hinted at a ferocious lover in Canada. Marj listens with the old rapture to Kate's telephone voice, "more purry, more seductive. Amazing to see," she says of herself, "how my body straightened, became ten years younger, my feet ceased drearily to shuffle, I danced, laughed, flew upstairs and downstairs." A thunderstorm was going on, and Winky, Marj's old Pekingese, climbed into her lap, trembling, and looked up at her for comfort.

Louise, Marianne's sister, telephones Marj: "Est-ce que tu es toujours amoureuse?" Marj answers, "Oui!" She is happy, alone with no sense of loneliness. "The silence here," she writes in her journal, "the birds are silent, the wind is silent, not a leaf moves in the still air. Yesterday they flew up and down in the rain like the keys of a player piano." Kinds of silence. Kate's silence about her operation, her letters, in which there was nothing of her true feelings. Protecting me or protecting herself? Marj's mind races backwards before she falls asleep. She dreams that she is being berated by a woman who follows her everywhere, whose diatribe goes on and on, who shakes her finger. "I'm glad to wake up," she writes in her journal. Her friends in Florida would say, "The woman is yourself."

Marj looks from her studio window and freezes. A doe is standing in the long grass, her head up, her eyes fixed on Marj. She licks her lips, puts up her nose and sniffs the air, and stamps her exquisite black foot—a peremptory stamp—repeated. Her narrow face, her big mobile ears are like a kangaroo's. She bends her head for a mouthful of grass, then turns, unfrightened, and bounds, leisurely soaring and falling down past the bunchy wild apple tree. "Today," Marj writes, "heat and heavenly stillness." She feels a weightless happiness, she would like to dance to her own waltzing thoughts, the memory in her own body of the doe's airborne flight. That night she dreams of seeing Lenny, Kate's actress-friend. She feels happy, puts her arms around her and kisses her face. Lenny looks a bit uncomfortable. In the process of kissing her, Marj has stepped on one of Lenny's feet. "A memory," Marj writes, "of her white stockings and little black Mary Jane pumps."

Marj's dreams reflect her life, with "a little worm of uncertainty," as she calls it, at their heart. The collage of Kate and Lenny, of Marj dancing with each and stepping on her feet, the dream-image of Marj kissing Lenny, a stand-in for Kate? Marj and Kate have been discussing sex in their letters—Kate has had misgivings about her "performance." But before they met they had agreed that the outcome did not matter—"orgasms are not compulsory," wrote Kate and Marj laughed with joy and relief. Sex would not be a source of hurt feelings or guilt; their old age would protect them against taking it too seriously. The word "performance" struck a dissonant note; it suggested a success or failure of technique (Marj thinks of tennis again)—the correct angle of the wrist, placement of strokes, scores, rallies, etc. Kate has the carpal tunnel syndrome in one wrist and will be given an injection of cortisone before coming to Canada. Marj reminds Kate of the limitations of her own enthusiasm for sex. "When we talk on the telephone," she says, "I feel such warm, loving contentment and ease, as if we're sitting on your blue sofa with our arms around each other, not saying, 'Let's jump into bed this very second'; we love each other just as we did when we met at the airport—the foregone conclusion that doesn't conclude. I've told you many times before that *only* your body could create my sense of safety, sureness of your instant knowledge of how to respond or how to initiate. It amazes me, too, that I can assume without a sense of hubris that you feel the same way about me." Marj takes the tensile strength of their physical bond too much for granted—what she can safely say to Kate, the words she can use. Her words which seem as clear as day to her, reflect her wish, like Kate's in the domain of logic, to "make things ABSOLUTELY RIGHT in their relationship." Sex will take care of itself, she thinks, since their language for it cannot be misunderstood. Hadn't Kate written that neither was more demanding than the other? And added with wonderful assurance, "We'll be talking and laughing *together* again soon"?

Chapter Seven

Marj is waiting at the Vancouver airport, a mirror image of Kate at the Sydney airport at the time of their first meeting. In the sister city, the spruce trees are as tall and straight as Australian eucalyptus, the harbour, like Sydney Harbour, is swarming with craft of every kind, crisscrossing the blue-dancing water. In Vancouver, a backdrop of snow-topped mountains outdoes the Sydney scenic view, Marj thinks with satisfaction. Surely, she thinks, this flawless day will recall to Kate the day they first met, and will repeat its joy. She has conveniently erased memories of difference in their letters, the fact that neither is absolutely right from the point of view of the other, and that Kate has written that the traumas of her former visits to Canada have made her anxious about this one. "Could it happen again?" A query by Kate that dampened Marj's spirits.

Marj has rented a cottage for a week at Seawrack, an idyllic little peninsula attached to Saltspring Island, clasped on either side by the Gulf. Each cottage bears the name of a celebrated woman radical; theirs is Rosa Luxembourg. Marj has been told that she and Kate are likely to see otters climbing sinuously over the rocks, and eagles stationed on the treetops. She says to herself, quoting Kate, "We'll be talking and laughing together *soon.*"

Marj's daydreams are arrested when the arrival door flies open and Kate emerges, pushing a baggage-wagon piled high with luggage. She is dressed all in black with a scarlet tie, like a narrow fall of molten lava, knotted loosely around her neck. Her eyes are bloodshot, her face is taut and pale, she hasn't slept for twenty-three hours, she says after their perfunctory embrace. Fear flares in Marj. There will be no time for Kate to rest; they must take a taxi immediately to the dock to catch their ferry. Marj has not considered the logistics of moving heavy suitcases, of moving their combined luggage onto the first ferry without help. She has forgotten the fragility of Kate's wrist, still painful from the carpal tunnel syndrome, and the possibility that Kate may still be recuperating from her operation.

In the taxi Marj takes Kate's lifeless hand and lets it drop. Kate has discovered that Marj does not know if there will be porters on the ferry dock. Kate's big suitcase, which they can barely lift between them, is standing upright next to the driver, the trunk is full and bags are squeezed around their feet. "Annie is meeting us at the first ferry dock and will help with the bags," says Marj. She thinks tenderly of Annie, the poet, who has been able to imagine two old women, one of them exhausted, lugging bags across the vast distances that separate ferries from taxis. Annie is an experienced islander, young and strong. "Annie will help us," says Marj, certain that Kate will share her confidence. "Are you sure that Annie will be there?" Kate asks sharply. "Have you agreed on a place to meet?" Marj's mind begins a panicky scattering, like frightened sheep. Has she accurately remembered what Annie said on the telephone? Will Annie be at the dock where Marj and Kate change to the Saltspring ferry or at the dock on Saltspring when they arrive? "I've written it down somewhere," she says to Kate, fumbling in vain among the scraps of paper in her handbag.

Getting aboard the ferry is more difficult than Marj's worst imagined scenarios. The two of them, with frequent stops for rest, carry their bags along the passageway and up two flights of steps on the ferry; they dump them higgledy-piggledy in a corner. Marj hurries off to the purser's office and implores the woman purser to find someone to get their bags on to the dock at the next stop; a grumpy man appears and staggers with them to an unknown destination. Kate is waiting for Marj in the lounge. "I felt sorry for you just now, Marj," she says, "when you were running around looking for someone to help. Your face was bright red." This calm appraisal strongly suggests to Marj that in her place Kate would have used logic to arrange for a porter to help them with their bags. But Kate is suddenly silent, attentively smiling. Two scholarly-looking women have introduced themselves to Marj and are baling her up. They loved the film she was in, they say. They exchange addresses and telephone numbers.

When the two friendly women have moved away, Kate says to Marj, "I've never been so badly treated in my life." She tells Marj that she has been thoughtless, incompetent and irresponsible. "You agree, don't you?" she asks. "You understand why?" It occurs to Marj that Kate is comparing her welcome for Marj in Australia with Marj's slapdash preparations for Kate's arrival in Vancouver. Kate had risen at dawn, driven to the airport to meet Marj; she had put together a mixture of comfort, relaxation, lunch, a walk down to the harbour, and a nap for the traveller—all perfectly orchestrated. In this similar place, breathtakingly beautiful, Marj should have (she imagines Kate thinking) shown the same respect for Kate that Kate had for her. She should have rolled out the red carpet instead of leaving so many important details to chance. Perhaps Kate is maddened by the fact that Marj is willing to endure the horrors of this day; she seems to expect Kate to do the same, and to be a good sport about her painful wrists and her exhaustion; it shows how little Marj thinks about Kate's welfare. "I'm sorry," says Marj. It seems to infuriate Kate that Marj is sorry; sorriness will do nothing to change Marj's nature, which, as Kate points out, is arrogant and self-centred.

In a less humble part of herself, Marj is not sorry at all. Her body chemistry has changed as it did during the logic sessions, her wits are dull, the grey matter of her brain is inert fluff, her blood is embalming fluid. She is angry with Kate for training her attention on her when they could both be vibrating to the deep hum of the engine under their feet; they could take heart from the blueness of the water steadily sliding past them, the shifting, hazy silhouettes of distant islands.

When Kate and Marj change ferries for the trip to Saltspring Island the purser tells them that their bags will be waiting on the lower dock. They are there, huddled in a lonely cluster, but Kate and Marj are the only passengers disembarking and Annie is nowhere to be seen. So this isn't the place where we're supposed to meet, Marj thinks despairingly; it must be the dock at Saltspring. She will learn too late that Annie, having faithfully fulfilled her promise, has been on the upper deck where passengers disembark—waiting and searching, and that she has missed the ferry to Saltspring. Out in the hot sun, in the air fragrant with sea smells, mingled with the tarry perfume of the dock, Kate relaunches her case against Marj with new evidence that Marj has got it wrong again, for now Marj can't remember precisely anything that Annie said. Annie will be angry with me, too, Marj thinks, dropping under the imagined weight of two angers. A crazy hope enters her mind: Annie will be at Saltspring to greet us, for in her meltdown of forgetfulness she is able to imagine the impossible. She conjures up a real-life image of Annie standing on the dock, wearing khaki shorts, a faded lavender T-shirt, of her boyish smiling face under a shock of yellow hair. A long boardwalk connects the ferry dock at Saltspring to the island. Annie is not there. Marj leaves Kate with the bags while she walks to find the nearest telephone to call for a taxi. At this moment her luck turns; she is recognized by a woman who has seen her film, who offers to help with the bags and to take Kate and Marj to Rosa Luxembourg. Their new friend, who seems to know Seawrack well, tells them that Emma Goldman is next door and that the two log cabins are perched over a rocky beach. When they arrive at Seawrack she carries Kate's big bag up the steps with muscular ease.

Dark water laps on the beach, stirred by a chilly off-shore breeze. Rosa L. is sparsely furnished, with neither a TV nor a telephone; Kate will sleep in the bedroom, Marj in the sofa bed in the living room. The cabins have been built and furnished with the assumption of loving relationships between their women tenants, and their acceptance of spartan simplicity. They must love nature, must freeze in silent reverence at the sight of the eagle who has chosen a lookout at the top of a dead tree, perches there in the sunlight turning its snowy head this way and that, screeches and takes off with strong wingbeats. Marj, on her way to the office to telephone, sees the eagle, and her spirits lift a little. She wishes that the eagle would carry away the incubus that sits on her as she makes her way through the pink-gold grass. An awkward, inept self inhabits her, she barges by mistake into the manager's kitchen and has to be taught how to use the cordless telephone. She talks to Diana who tells her that Annie is on her way to Saltspring, that she waited a long time at the first dock, with the hope that Kate and Marj would show up on the next ferry from Vancouver.

Marj does not want Kate to discover that Annie has waited for more than two hours at the first ferry dock. "Annie and Diana are coming to see us tomorrow," she responds to Kate's questioning look. Rosa Luxembourg is in deep shade now and a cool wind from the inlet is blowing through the open front door. There is nothing to do except eat a meagre supper and go to bed. Kate's anger has revived and rises to a crescendo. She suddenly stops shouting and writes at length in her journal. "Do you want to read my impressions of the day? I don't want you to read it if you're not going to pay attention to what I say." "I'd like to read it," says Marj. She reads a minute-by-minute account of the day, a log, without any hint of discord or a suggestion of Kate's anger. "Well?" says Kate. "It's a straightforward record of the day," says Marj. "What we *did*." "Doesn't it say anything to you about your behaviour?" "You've already told me about my behaviour," says Marj. "You were crystal clear. I've already apologized." "I don't want you to apologize!" Kate is in full cry again. "I want you to understand! You don't understand!"

The manager has told Marj that a couple of women are staying in Emma Goldman. Perhaps they are lying in each other's arms, Marj thinks. Perhaps they suspend their love-making when one of them says, "It's beginning again." In the night sky a full moon, a lovers' moon, casts a benign light over the log cabins. Kate is crying that she has news for Marj. Her amazing voice, trained by Terry Grant, the consonants and diphthongs perfectly articulated, is borne past Emma Goldman, to the end of the peninsula, where a couple of otters are playing on the rocks. Moonlight glances off their wet coats. Kate is heating up her sense of outrage in Rosa Luxembourg. It will grow and flourish for the duration of her visit until they face each other in an insect's universe where stiff grass blades hang over them like swords of Damocles.

The next morning, in the chilly silence of breakfast time, Marj hears a car door close. Diana and Annie have come with Lakshmi to welcome Kate and Marj; they have brought raspberries from their garden and homemade cookies. Diana's foot is in a cast, her face is drawn with pain, but the arrival of the three friends transforms Kate and Marj; Kate's eyes turn bright blue and Marj feels joy spreading in her heart. Her marvellous friends have come against all odds, for their house is full of guests, they are giving a big party tomorrow, and Diana can only hobble on her crutches. They are shedding their attention, their affection like stardust on Kate and Marj, who for the time of their visit will be, briefly, transformed. When they leave, Kate, with a spontaneous gesture of thoughtfulness, sends Marj and Lakshmi off for a walk while she busies herself in the log cabin.

Lakshmi is wearing a raspberry-coloured shirt, corduroy trousers and sturdy leather shoes. Marj studies her face, tenderly grave, and her dark brown eyes, and is soothed by the melody of her deep voice. "Kate has been reading me the Riot Act," Marj says. ("To declare authoritatively that a course of action, or conduct must cease," Marj will read in the dictionary.) "Well, Marj," says Lakshmi, "don't you think that it's high time that someone read you the Riot Act?" Marj is not offended; she has heard the grace note of humour that makes Lakshmi's speech so caressing. "Yes, of course, but…I'm not that awful." As they trudge toward the end of the peninsula, she hears herself babbling to Lakshmi, with a glad sense of freedom, and bursts of pent-up laughter. For it is a comedy, isn't it, her beautiful visit to Kate in Australia, its smooth-running perfection, turned into an object-lesson to show her her own insufficiencies? The inevitable comparison between the Australian hostess with her professional standards and her Canadian counterpart who has been unable to imagine Kate's high expectations as a guest. All Marj's goodwill, the plans she *has* made, now strike her as ludicrously inadequate. It is true, she says to Lakshmi, that she messed up Kate's arrival, that her planning was sloppy, that she had not used logic to solve logistic problems, but are these reasons for Kate to be so continuously furious? It will occur to her eventually that perhaps Kate is furious because Marj doesn't love her enough to put herself in her skin, and that her self-esteem is reduced by the haphazard dimensions of Marj's welcome. Walking slowly along with Lakshmi, Marj knows only that, away from Kate, the burden of Kate's fury slips off her and she can laugh again. Meantime, Lakshmi has been silent, looking soberly at the ground. Then she murmurs, "Things are bound to get better, Marj. Kate is tired and cranky from her trip." They have walked out of the woods into strong sunshine, they are bathed in its light, warming them, forming frail patterns on the restlessly moving grass. The dancing blue water is beyond, and arbutus trees grow close to the rocky edge of the peninsula. Their trunks are like the spring antlers of a stag, a vivid blood-red; under their peeling bark the young branches are freshly green.

Marj's sight is restored, her turgid senses come to life, she is aware of how much her attention is deadened when Kate's scrutiny is trained on her. During their first evening in Rosa Luxembourg Kate said with misleading candour, "You didn't enjoy the day much either, did you?" Marj wanted to answer, "It was horrible!" but she answered carefully, "It didn't give me much pleasure." She was surprised that there was enough material in this to rekindle Kate's rage. "It didn't give you much pleasure! There you go again whinging. Me! Me! Me!" "My mother-in-law is the whingingest person on the face of the earth," said the man in the grocery store near Kate's apartment in Sydney. Marj remembers how this made her laugh inwardly. On the dock, she thinks, Kate would have had the same reaction if Marj had said, "I enjoyed every

111

minute of the day." "Me! Me! Me!" Kate could have said, and added, "What about me?"

At bedtime they do not exchange even perfunctory kisses. Their only cooperative act in Rosa Luxembourg is to wrestle open the sofa bed before Kate vanishes into the bedroom. She has told Marj at supper that she knows that she is egocentric and arrogant, doesn't she? Marj wishes she could make one of the several possible replies that churn sluggishly in her head. It is uncharacteristic of her to be so bereft of answers: sarcastic, cutting, deftly insulting—the sort she used to make in her quarrels with Marianne in championship matches which honed their vocabularies and repartee. She remembers that when Marianne accused her of having once been sensitive but of having turned into a frigid didactic feminist, she hurled back, "You're a little Napoleon, a megalomaniac!" The sting of the word "frigid" lingered for a long time, yet it was the kind of liberating quarrel which could fizzle away in laughter the next day. After a ritual period of mutual stiffness, of course. But Marj and Kate can no longer find solace in laughter, or exchange tentative healing smiles.

Marj tosses and turns on the sofa bed; the shades are sucked violently against the windows by the night breeze. The next morning at breakfast Marj is silent. Kate's look is cool and quizzical; she seems to be waiting for Marj to say something, but Marj is unable to say anything that Kate might like to hear. She goes off with Annie with a treacherous lifting of her spirits, to the lively little town, as exciting to Marj after the rigours of Seawrack as a big city. Her own elasticity surprises her, her effervescence when she talks to Annie, with whom she can discuss all the paradoxes of human nature. Does Annie, too, suffer from the huge oscillations that can reduce Marj's power to love to zero?

Marj's conversation with Annie moves allegro con moto, without the need for laboured explanation or any room for misunderstanding. They are sitting on upturned barrels, sipping big bowls of café au lait in the shade of the grapevine overhead while the day sparkles out on the sunny street. And Marj is struck once again by the delightful paths friendship can take compared to the briar-choked thickets of love. She and Kate, too, had skipped along those paths before they met, and after they met, in beautiful sanctuaries.

Annie drives Marj back to Seawrack and Kate welcomes them with newborn brightness. She wants them to hear her news. She has cast her spell over the otters at the point, they have succumbed to her softly seductive voice, just as Oliver does in Australia, bowing his head, twining his lithe grey and white body around Kate's legs. The otters looked at her, Kate says, saw a fellow creature, and went on playing. This magical event has softened her look at Marj.

The party is tonight, the poetic work of the two poets, Diana and Annie. It is partly to honour the bond between Marj and Kate, partly, though Marj does not know it yet, to express a farewell to the island by Diana and Annie and to the beauty of their life together. They will sell their house and go their separate ways, with a new life for each, fulfilling the lesbian destiny by which women are born into their future lives while they are still living this one. They will know the rending pain of division, the pre-condition for being reborn.

Annie makes yet another trip to Seawrack to fetch Kate and Marj for the party. They are welcomed by Damian, the official mascot, who unfolds his long legs and pushes his bony thin-skinned head under their hands in greeting. The faithful dog who recognized Odysseus after his years of wandering must have had the noble look of Damian, the hollows above his far-seeing yellow eyes, the tender droop at the corners of his mouth. Brightness is falling from the air, the day in its long exit blends with darkness and soft air, still warm from the sun. The guests inside are happy. The party is in the tradition of great feasts. In the middle of the dining room table is a silver bowl full of roses from the garden, tinged with pink and apricot, exhaling an intoxicating sweetness. Kate, wearing a flowing peacock-blue shirt and black pants, has bloomed, her face is pink, her eyes are splendidly blue. (But Diana has a fine line of pain between her eyebrows and sits with her leg stretched out, her foot in plaster.) Marj catches Kate's challenging eye, which seems to say, "You love me now, don't you?" and Marj smiles at her. She is clowning a little, making her comical gestures, charming the guests, doing it, too, for herself and Marj. She might be saying, as she did in Australia, when she placed herself in front of Marj and struck a seductive pose, "When you look at me, doesn't it make you wild with desire?" She was playing Sally in *Cabaret*, with Sally's appeal, half-mocking, that made Kate so adorable in Marj's eyes. At the party, Marj shifts her eyes away from Kate, she does not feel love coming to her rescue as it used to. Is Kate playing the lover now, fully aware of her audience, is she inviting Marj to join her as her happy partner? Does she want herself and Marj to appear as the perfect couple? Marj is aware of a cold undercurrent of wariness in herself. She no longer feels the urge to fall into Kate's arms, right there in front of everybody, or shout into the night, "Kate and I are lovers!" She and Kate have not touched each other since Kate arrived, since they have been together in the secret world where each is absolutely alone.

At a future time Kate will reproach Marj for not having appreciated the hard work that went into her public performances. It was hard to look happy when she wasn't. Was it really hard work? Didn't she slip easily into the skin of the charismatic Kate who was genuinely happy? Before they met she described to Marj her pre-party excitement as a child, followed by pure delight. There must still be a solid stratum in Kate of that delight, Marj thinks.

Back in Rosa Luxembourg, Kate and Marj are alone with each other again and the spell of the party is wearing off. It is as though both of them have been kidnapped by Pluto, the old spoilsport, and imprisoned in the gloom of Hades. Perhaps the cabin is haunted by Rosa herself, who lived and died for justice, and exchanged a comfortable life for one of danger and austerity. How can happy lesbian couples be expected to live under the spell of Rosa, Emma and the other great revolutionary women, without pangs of guilt? Perhaps the simplicity of the log cabins is meant to remind them of Rosa's and Emma's indifference to material things. Marj's sense of well-being would have responded better, she thinks, to Virginia Woolf or Willa Cather. Either one of them would have made the cabin more welcoming, either one would have received Kate and Marj as kindred spirits and made them feel at home just as Marj's friends did. Rosa, who would perhaps have used the cottage as a hiding place, would have had no use for Kate and Marj with their bourgeois craving for comfort and their timidity in the face of danger. Marj had fallen in love with the woman who played the part of Rosa in the movie, she wept copiously when Rosa was killed and her body was thrown off a bridge into the swift-moving river below. But Marj would never have had the courage to be one of Rosa's comrades; and she feels now like someone Rosa would have despised. She is alone with Kate, whom Rosa, after all, might perhaps have admired, at moments when Kate's entire body was electric with anger. Rosa, too, was fired with a passionate sense of the justice of her cause.

During the week at Seawrack, Kate relaxes with Marj's friends, who know so surely how to live beautifully, but when she and Marj are alone again, they are unable to move toward each other, the magnetic waves that connected them in Australia are jammed, they speak to each other with false politeness. Kate seems to study Marj with distaste, and get her into sharp focus. Why is Marj going on this way about the incomparable virtues of her friends and how much they admire Kate? "They're *your* friends," says Kate. "They're nice to me because of you." Kate is extinguishing her own pleasure, denying that Marj is in any way responsible for it or that the friends like Kate for her own sake. The peerless friends, their fidelity each to each, the beauty of their houses and landscapes, should act as object lessons to Kate and Marj, but are a hidden bone of contention. For Marj, too, comes to life with them and sheds her burden of gloom. To Kate, perhaps, she seems to be saying, "This is how *we* could be but you've made it impossible." Perhaps Kate reads Marj's sudden gaiety as a preference: "I like my friends better than I like you." After the party Marj throws for Kate in Montreal Kate will say, "Your friends laugh at my jokes but you're bored out of your silly mind."

One might suppose that Marj's friends in Canada would play the same role as Kate's friends in Australia. Their kindness and hospitality is a mirror image of the welcome extended to Marj by Kate's friends. That pattern has not changed; the change is in the interior of Kate's mind. Here in Canada she is no longer directing the action; she is at the mercy of Marj's deficiencies, which took shape at the moment of their meeting in Vancouver and will grow exponentially until they part in Montreal. Marj imagines the roiling of anxiety in Kate's mind, her confused sense of herself as the person who is used to controlling the action but who is now expected to exist as a kind of satellite.

116

At the end of the week, Kate and Marj leave Seawrack and take a ferry to Galiano, another glorious island. They fall into the arms of friends again, the warming beams of their kindness, in the exemplary house with its view over massed spruces and firs, out to glassy water and to other islands. Inside the house, they enjoy the comfort, the harmony and order that mirrors Kate's dream; there are West Coast paintings on the walls, the very best, that the friends have chosen, and drinks on the dot of 5:30. So far in British Columbia no friends have failed to show respect for this ritual—"the companionable sitting-together, the exchange of ideas," as Kate wrote to Marj in her defence of booze. Kate is visibly happy; she pours herself out to the magnificent friends, she has found space for herself. Marj's friends listen as Kate reels out the silken thread of her voice, the captivating voice of a born speaker. They all look at a video about May Sarton, whose mind strikes sparks, whose beautiful old face is alive with her passion for being. "I want to make old age into a work of art," she says. Sarton's life, like Kate's, left room for anger, for furies against people she loved. She read them the Riot Act, and they understood because they loved her. Out of her poured the mitigating flood of her oeuvre; anger was the dross left over from creation. Perhaps like Kate she needed anger and a worthy object of it, someone whose offence she thought would exonerate her. The creation of the offence is a work of art in itself.

The friends have planned visits to other houses near the silver-glittering sea, to women who are bound to each other, comfortable together. The couples on their islands appear to have found places that further their "soulmate-ship," Kate's word for her relationship with Marj. (It was her hope, she said in a pre-Canada letter, that logic would reveal Marj's moral values and her political philosophy, would uncover their compatibilities and incompatibilities and further their "soulmateship.") Marj and Kate are taken to have dinner with another ideal couple who live in a house high above the water. It is late afternoon and the fiery disc of the sun is low in the sky. Marj wonders how she and Kate appear to the others. As another couple like themselves? Isn't each playing her public role as soulmate to the other? Marj is studying the woman whom Marj had imagined (before her meeting with Kate) as Kate's double, who is now looking at Kate, and says, "You look like my mother." Now she is revealed to Marj as someone who does not look like Kate but whose mother looks like Kate. A step backward in time, a new unfathomable identity. This wonderfully merry woman lives with an apparent soulmate, warm and wise, and both appear to be beyond any possibility of serious difference. They have discovered their time being and live in it, like the two friends who brought Kate and Marj to see them. But what is Kate thinking? Does she think that she is on stage again, playing herself as heroine, playing soulmateship with Marj? Is she playing the beguiling Kate as object lesson to Marj? Is she thinking, Marj and I could live happily in this kind of place, in this ideal way? Ever since she arrived in Canada she has been shown ideal ways that other women have chosen. Is she thinking, if Marj would only change in the ways I've suggested, if she could be more like her friends, we might be happy in Canada?

The women are standing on the balcony, beckoned by the red gaze of the sun. They hear a cry from below, "Look at me! Look at me!" They look directly down at the dancing leaves of an apple tree and the dark head and brown limbs of a little boy, who pulls himself from branch to branch until his head emerges, his mouth crying, "Look at me!" His face is triumphantly tipped up toward the women who make him feel heroic, who do not scold him when his wish to be naughty turns him into a demon, and are now crying in answer, "Julian! We see you!" They are a little anxious, since, even so far above Julian, they can hear the swish of leaves and the snapping of small branches. They are all linked together by their autonomous lives and their self-assurance as tender aunts. They leave their posts only when Julian and his embracing tree are lost in deep shade and the burning eye of the sun has sunk into the water.

Chapter Eight

At the literary festival on the Sunshine Coast, Marj is one of the speakers and Kate is again in the uncomfortable position of satellite. It is their first conference together, a new test for each—for Marj, of her ability to remember the important existence of a partner at her side; for Kate, a painful test, for she doesn't know a soul and depends on Marj to introduce her. Marj sometimes forgets. The festival participants are a mixed group of men and women writers, husbands and wives and a few lesbians. Marj feels paralyzed by shyness, she feels homesick for the familiar faces at the book fair in Amsterdam, the swirling of women happy to see each other, spontaneous embraces and their ease of communication. The cobblestoned streets and outdoor tables, restaurants and museums were meeting places, tributaries leading to and from the great meeting hall. Hundreds of women were talking and listening to each other there, with a sense that they could set the world on fire. Sometimes they were crowded into rooms too small to hold them and sat on the floor; Marj remembers a Greek poet and an Argentine poet seated in front of her, leaning against her raised knees, while the Greek poet gently massaged the kinks out of her friend's neck and shoulders.

In Amsterdam, Marj and the South African woman activist, Ellen Kuzwayo, met to discuss their talk together.

"I don't know what we're going to talk about," said Ellen. "What shall we say?" "Well, we're both old," Marj said. "That's it!" said Ellen, "We'll talk about being old!" So they talked about being old, about their meeting four years before at the Women's Book Fair in Montreal, when each talked about memory and how every woman's memory adds to the remembered chronicle of women's history. From then on, whenever they met in Amsterdam they threw their arms around each other's necks with the effervescent affection that bubbled between them all.

The Festival of the Living Arts was created by women with a dream of an inclusive celebration, men and women of all artistic persuasions, novelists, poets, radio show-people, playwrights. The site is close to the little town of Sechelt and to the dazzling sea that breaks on the shores of the Sunshine Coast. Everybody in Sechelt has pitched in to help, and the festival has thrived. Kate and Marj are taken under the wing of one of the founders and her husband, who has volunteered to shuttle participants from their motel up the road to the Festival. The founder is wearing a silk wind-jacket and pants the colour of her eyes—forget-me-not blue; they both have silvery hair like the silver afternoon sea; they are a paradigmatic couple, powerful citizens bien dans leur peaux. Her beautiful blue wind-suit, his clean khaki pants and madras shirt, their snowy running shoes are paradigmatic, too. Underneath these outer skins lies the mystery of each of them which neither will divulge. They are not in the habit, as lesbians are, of baring their souls at a first meeting. Marj recognizes them as the perfect people she admired long ago—discreet, warm-hearted and kind with a recognizable North American kindness. Long ago at debutante parties, Marj knew that she would never be a perfect person even if she had learned how to be a nice girl who could draw men out. She would never have the required self-assurance; she would always speak with the detectable accent of an outsider. Marj notices how comfortable Kate looks with their guardian angels, how well, how charmingly she speaks the inflected language of social graces, how she is never at a loss for words or for some bit of action that will make people laugh.

Kate and Marj have been billeted up the road from the Festival in a motel where they are given a room with twin beds. It is the first time since they met that they have shared a room. They are stuck with each other in close quarters; they turn their backs on each other when they dress for dinner; they eat together in the dining room and hardly exchange a word. The other people there show no eagerness to talk to them. Marj thinks, they can't be part of the Festival; she feels vaguely guilty, conscious of Kate's discontent, her expressionless face which Marj interprets as, what are we supposed to do here, stuck in a motel miles from the Festival with people we don't know? The Festival events don't begin until tomorrow. Kate and Marj go to bed early like two strangers, and the next morning both are cranky. "I couldn't sleep because you were snoring," says Marj. "You snore, too," says Kate. On the way to the Festival, they stop at a drugstore and buy earplugs, which will turn out to be ineffectual.

At the Festival, Marj feels more shy than ever. Her speech is scheduled for the next day; today she and Kate listen to a novelist and to a poet reading their work; Marj recognizes a few friends. When she forgets to introduce Kate, Kate steps forward and says, "My name is Kate. I'm from Australia." She begins her saga of how she met Marj. She looks alive, her eyes sparkle like the sea, she has the ability to be instantly on friendly terms. Marj cannot think of a word to say to the well-known poet, nor to the world-celebrated novelist who looks like a cornered animal. Marj is aware of isolated souls, of singular anxieties—recognizable people who are looking for familiar faces, and have trouble swimming in this sea of strangers. The rules for mingling here, different from the melting pot in Amsterdam, have to do with discretion, not making friends too hastily or with everybody, with holding oneself a little aloof. But the reckless, fearless rushing toward each other of women in Amsterdam had followed the dynamics of an all-women conference. At a mixed conference the women are sharply aware of every man and his power to draw them closer. Marj with Kate feels super-aware of being a woman-couple in a place where there are hardly any others. She realizes, too, that Kate is better able than she to cross into the world of men and women. Kate relaxes, sure of her own power, she bales up the male novelists and poets, while Marj clams up, she can't think of anything to say. Her ease with the paradigmatic husband is the result of his friendly greeting.

Kate takes seriously the responsibilities of being half a couple, and Marj is not aware that as they stand in line in the morning for events like everybody else, Kate is assuming what she calls her "Pollyanna" persona, bequeathed to her by her mother—the irresistible desire and need to be useful, to solve "easy little problems of logic." In the evening she and Marj are spirited into the auditorium while the rest of the audience is still waiting outside. Marj doesn't want to have anything to do with this miracle, she wants to disassociate herself from Kate's thoughts for her welfare, which she reads in Kate's triumphant smile. She imagines a scene in which Kate has taken the beautiful founder into her confidence, a scene in which she hints at the frailties of old age. "Marj doesn't look her age," Kate says in Marj's imagination, "but she is seventy-six and standing is tiring for her. Perhaps you could arrange for her to go in ahead of the others?" Marj would prefer to look as though she were glad to share any discomfort with the others. She is reluctant to accept the perks of old age, and would rather wobble like a bowling pin about to fall than be helped over rough ground. She has observed this perverse pride in friends her own age. Marj is, besides, in her visceral dislike for complaining, a reversal of her mother who seemed to delight, at a restaurant, in sending soup back to the kitchen if it was lukewarm, or to summon the waitress and itemize the ways in which the dinner was bad. For Marj's mother it was a question of keeping restaurants on their toes, and demonstrating her own high standards.

The next day at the Festival, Kate is somewhere in the audience that comes to hear Marj's speech about the film. It is about being in the cast and an update of the seven other women in it; it is about their bright memories and how they were changed by being together for most of a summer. She tries to remember to speak slowly and clearly, but her hands holding the text of her speech are shaking. She has not spotted Kate but is aware of her presence, aware that what she is saying may strike Kate as a load of codswallop. For it is not always true that a group of women becomes a group of loving friends; sometimes they end up divided and angry. But even if the women in the film with Marj squabbled now and then off-camera, they met in a region beyond discord, a little island of felicity. They held title to it, they went there to recover their memories. They met, too, in a place where they were honoured as old women, in an oasis, protected from the uninhabitable deserts of old age. After Marj's speech she runs into one of yesterday's speakers, a woman broadcaster, known far and wide, who made her listeners laugh with delight. "You were fabulous!" she says to Marj. "*You* were fabulous!" says Marj.

Kate and Marj leave the Festival that afternoon, take the ferry to Horseshoe Bay and are met by Tony who has come from Vancouver to meet them and take them down the coast. Kate's charisma blooms, just as it did with

Martha, Marj's editor who drove them up to the Festival; Martha was immediately charmed by Kate, her quick wit and purring laughter and the Australian melody of her voice. Marj felt healed by the elixir, the steady love flowing between herself and Martha, potent enough to change Kate, the magic spell worked by Marj's Vancouver friends and her island friends, the lifting of her heart. With her friends there can be none of the sharp surprises of her time alone with Kate, when she no longer feels safe. Martha had contrived a smooth-running schedule for Kate and Marj that left nothing to chance; Marj cannot make a mistake when one of her friends is with her. When Martha left them to take the ferry to Sechelt, an anxious child cried out in Marj, "Don't leave us! Don't leave us alone together!" For as surely as in a fairy story when a happy spell is withdrawn, Kate would resume her case against Marj and Marj would become inert and loveless.

On the way to Vancouver in Tony's jeep, Tony and Marj and Kate are as gay as larks. Tony has bright dark eyes like a chipmunk and thick hair that falls over her forehead. In Vancouver she shepherds Kate and Marj to their hotel, they leave their bags and pick up Nora, Tony's partner, who works with handicapped children. She is sturdy, pink-cheeked; she and Tony seem to fit comfortably together in a non-competitive bond which gives each one equal power, each with eager interest in the splendid world around them. Like the Australians she met, Marj thinks, with their reverence for birds and animals. Tony parks the jeep and the four of them walk across Stanley Park through alternating patches of deep shade and phosphorescent moonlight where they see little spotted skunks—Tony points them out—running their nocturnal errands unafraid. They run with innocent purpose, disappear in the shade of the huge trees, and reappear as they enter the glowing moonlight, part of the enchantment that briefly softens Kate's and Marj's hearts. They are in the company of two young women full of goodwill and eager attention, who are treating them to lobster and red wine at the restaurant. When Kate goes to the restroom, Tony and Nora sing her praises, just as Martha had: "She's wonderful! I see why you fell in love." "Yes," says Marj, and when Kate comes back Marj says, "Tony and Nora have been singing your praises."

When they walk back across the park, Nora and Kate go ahead; Tony and Marj lag behind them. Marj is urgently impelled to talk to Tony about Kate's anger, how unexpectedly it flared up even in the joyful time in Australia, how for Kate it is not anger but a necessary expression of her passionate being, how for Marj it is intolerable aggression that reduces her to non-being. She tells Tony that she links Kate's fits of fury to drinkie-time—at least when she is alone with Marj. The other persona of drinkie-time is Kate's delightful self in company—"the way she is with you and Nora," says Marj. "Kate is a theatre-person," says Marj. "She plays herself with professional expertise." She tells Tony of the dramatic incident when Kate's memories seemed to take over her words and the movements of her body, how, leaning forward, she struck her left wrist hard with the fingers of her right hand. "I suppose I'm wrong again!" she cried. "Wrong! Wrong! Wrong!" A sharp blow like a karate chop by the punishing fingers on the helpless left wrist. "A play within a play," says Marj to Tony. "A replay of real punishment? She told me that she doesn't believe in punishment and has gotten rid of guilt; she believes that she's incapable of punishing anybody." Marj tells Tony that Kate had dreaded coming to Canada; she'd had a bad time on her other trips and was apprehensive about this one while she was still in Australia. "Can it happen again?" she'd wondered in a letter to Marj. She thought of Canada "as a not too friendly place."

Tony is sorry to hear all this; she thinks that Kate is charming and full of understanding, and that she and Marj are having a normal falling-out between lovers, who invariably have quarrels that lead to reconciliation. They arrive on the other side of the park without having found a solution. Kate and Nora are waiting for them and Kate gives Marj a questioning look. "What were you and Tony talking about?" she will ask Marj, back in their hotel room. "Oh," says Marj, "about how Tony is resigning her editorial job, how she wants to look for a job in Calgary, how she and Nora have to separate for a while. Those two are adorable, aren't they?" Marj is becoming expert at equivocation.

The next morning Kate and Marj fly to Montreal.

Chapter Nine

When they arrive in Montreal, Kate is as fragile as Venetian glass. The house is stifling from the August sun. Marj shows Kate the guest room, the little room next door where Kate might like to do her writing, the bathroom without a shower. They do not embrace when they cross the threshold, as they did in Australia. Their bodies do not move toward each other and Marj has given up any hope of being able to read Kate's mind. She is taken by surprise when Kate shows her the Quimper mug from the bathroom. "It has a crack in it," says Kate. Yes, a crack and a chip out of the rim; it was one of the beat-up objects that Marj mended and lovingly preserved. It held in it her four years in Brittany. Kate has blown her top. "What makes you think I can drink brandy and soda out of a mug? Have you ever *seen* anyone drink brandy and soda out of a mug?" "I didn't say—" Marj begins. "You *did* say—" What did she say? Kate has caught her again in one of her dense webs, the surprise and anger from which there is no escape. It will come to Marj later that the Quimper mug is an image of herself, a dream-image, with the weird exactness of dreams, cracked and imperfect—the absence in her of a fine sense of the proper use of things, above all, Kate's use of things. For Marj has forgotten that it is drinkie-time in Montreal; she is still on Vancouver time. Kate's indignation has to find an equivalent symbol—the mug with the mended handle, the crack, the chip out of the rim. "Have you ever *heard* of anyone drinking brandy and soda out of a mug?" *"You* proposed that *I* might.... *You* have the nerve to imply that *I* am the kind of person...." Once, in Australia, Kate explained to Marj that a vicar and his family were considered low-class by high-class people and high-class by low-class people, an uncomfortable no man's land where you never know where you stand. Privileged people like me can afford to be stingy, Marj thinks, with cracked china and frayed towels, a form of class-conscious arrogance. I was right to feel apprehensive about Kate's visit to Montreal, she thinks. Her friends on the west coast served drinks at the proper time with comfortable ceremony, they made the work of cooking an exquisite dinner seem effortless; they drew Kate into after-dinner conversation about books, teaching and theatre.

The country house will heal Kate's soul, Marj thinks; she will breathe the sweet smelling air over the mown fields, edged by forests and undulating hills. At twilight bats are dimly visible foraging for insects close to the house, and the cool green-blue signal lights of fireflies, rising and falling, dance against the slope behind the house. Summer guests always settle into a rhythm of content; they go off on long walks, they bring back wildflowers, rocks, mushrooms from the woods; or they lie in the sun and fall asleep with an open book upside down on the grass beside them. Sometimes after a thunderstorm they are rewarded by the vision of a double rainbow spanning the east with one foot resting on a field close by, a surreal light turning whatever it touches into beaten gold.

Marianne and the cats are there to greet Kate and Marj. Marianne is wearing short ragged shorts and a fuchsia-coloured shirt with rolled-up sleeves. Her sunburnt arms and legs are thin and muscular, her face is pale, sheltered from the sun by tousled hair and a floppy grass-green hat. Kate greets Marianne like an old friend; she has come to life. And indeed, Marianne is a life raft for both Kate and Marj. Marianne and Kate have hit it off, just as Marj had foreseen.

Marianne has put flowers in Kate's room, heavy-headed white hydrangea and purple phlox on the dining room table. At supper, dazzled by Kate's joyful persona, Marianne pours glass after glass of wine for the two of them while Kate's voice unreels its long melody; Marianne is listening, spellbound. Marj goes to bed early; the sounds of Kate's dreamy narrative and of Marianne's intermittent answers travel through the floor of Marj's room and prevent her from sleeping.

The next morning Marianne leaves for Montreal and Kate and Marj are left together, not to throw their arms around each other's necks but to look at each other without pleasure. Marj knows that Marianne's magic spell will hold only as long as she is there. Without her, Kate is left alone with Marj, a virtual teetotaller who does not know how to plan meals or make the best use of their time together. Kate is left with the option of planning meals herself or letting Marj do it according to her casual lights. She will have to remind Marj to put soda water or wine on the list; otherwise she will forget. Kate has discovered that Marj, left to her own devices, seldom buys meat, and that the hearty and delicious meals Kate prepared in Australia have failed to suggest similar ones in Canada. But at least she can make changes in the diets of the cats. In no time, William, the grey senior cat, is dancing a sarabande around Kate's legs, bewitched just like Oliver. "Cats like to be needed," Kate says, a hint to Marj that both cats and people need to be liked. Her scenes with the cats are plays within plays; Kate in her attention to them, her flow of cat-talk, the cat food that appears by magic when they flock to the sound of her voice, suggest to Marj that she should indulge Kate just as Kate indulges the cats. But the more Marj feels Kate's sharp gaze on her, the less she is capable of harnessing her will for the effort that true hospitality requires.

In the morning Marj goes to her studio and sits looking fixedly at a faraway tree that has already begun to turn red. She senses that Kate would have liked to spend the morning, with Marj as attentive audience, by continuing to narrate what she has called "the huge substance" of her life. Marj's hope has been that each would be free to do her own work in solitude—Marj still making notes for her joyful first chapter, Kate working at her fictional autobiography, an ironic look at a somewhat irresolute woman named Frances. Marj is already acquainted with Frances and likes looking at Kate through the lens of her vision of herself. Frances, according to Kate, wonders if she does not prefer failure to success. She has tantrums and decides that on the whole she likes to have an audience for them. So far in Frances's story Kate seems to have screened out both her own beauty and her most likable qualities.

In the afternoon Kate gives Marj a shopping list and Marj goes to the nearby town and buys Kate the hamburger, tomatoes and onions she needs for her boeuf Bolognese. On the way home she adds twelve ears of corn, picked that morning—a treat, she thinks. Kate looks at the corn with disbelief. Is it meant to be eaten at the beginning of dinner, she asks, or with the boeuf Bolognese? Marj realizes that Kate's cooking schedule has been completely disrupted; she is a perfectionist and cares passionately about the balance of nutrients; the mismatching of corn on the cob with boeuf Bolognese is a distraction from her pièce de résistance. Marj leaves the bag of corn in the garage. After supper Kate says, "Would you like to know how those ears of corn made me feel? They made me feel as though I'd been slapped across the face with a dead fish." Is she making a joke? No, for her face is serious. She has discovered an exact equivalent for how she feels; she wants Marj to know that it was not like being slapped with twelve ears of corn but with the thud of one dead fish. In the language of exaggerated feelings, when one is in a state of extreme vulnerability, dream-images crowd the threshold between sleep and waking, a place of violence where one perceives violent images as real as reality. Strange translations of similar objects take place: twelve ears of corn, as dense as quasars, become a single dead (and deadly) fish. The stuff of dreams is the material for waking life.

How has it happened, Marj wonders, that she doesn't do anything right, that she does everything wrong with such inspired wrongness, as if she is trying to mock Kate with her behaviour, which has required the malfunction-ing of her brain, hands, feet, eyes? She thinks about her habits, shaped and hardened in the course of a lifetime; they anchor each day, they are compass points. In Australia Marj sank into Kate's comfortable habits; she got up later, she went to bed later, she ate more than she did at home, she even had a baby-size drinkie. "No more than fourteen drops," she told Kate, hoping that the fourteen drops would give Kate the sense that Marj was trying to share her life. Marj's modest steps along Kate's habit-paths perhaps appeared to Kate to be changing Marj for the good, toward a more hedonistic view of life, away from puritanism. But during the months before Kate came to Canada, Marj returned to her habits and her severe schedule, which, she believes, keeps the slackness of old age at bay. Now, she thinks, Kate has come, expecting to find traces of the easygoing habits she has planted in Marj, an acknowledgment of her sensible advice to relax and enjoy life, and instead finds that Marj has shed every bit of her influence and has renounced her image of the good life. Worse still, she is expected to live according to Marj's habits, to her indifference to real comfort, her carelessness about food, planned menus and shopping. Perhaps it depresses her to see how selfishly Marj is herself, unchanged by love; she doesn't realize that Kate's habits have been a gift of love.

Kate's nerves are stretched taut and snap unexpectedly. Why does Marj keep jumping up in the middle of a meal? Marj has left the table abruptly to get a fork, sugar, to let a cat in or a cat out, to show Kate something in a book, to change a CD. "DON'T GET UP AGAIN," says Kate. She stretches out her arm, clamps a strong hand around Marj's wrist and forces Marj slowly down to her chair. Marj has been jumping up and down to escape Kate's terrible scrutiny, her attention to Kate has been wandering. "Don't forget me like that," says Kate's grip on Marj's wrist. "Isn't what I'm saying more important than the cats?"

Marj has noticed that Kate sometimes looks frightened, as though Marj's shortcomings are a signal to her of some grave illness that is changing Marj's personality. "I'm worried about you, Marj," Kate said while they were still in Montreal. Marj is worried about herself. Is she getting Alzheimer's disease? She considers her panics of forgetfulness as possible symptoms; she remembers Joanne Woodward in *Rachel, Rachel,* and her growing panic as she runs from floor to floor of a parking garage, looking for her car. Like many old people, Marj is overly concerned with possible symptoms, all of which seem to be confirmed by the information in her medical encyclopedia. She doesn't discuss any of her fears with Kate, afraid that Kate, instead of saying firmly, "Nonsense!" will suggest an appointment with a neurologist.

Kate herself is in a state in which details are hugely magnified, when a chipped mug can signify insult and summarize Marj's thoughtlessness, when the unexpected appearance of corn on the cob is an affront to Kate's rules for right living. In Australia, Kate's sense of self is gently caressed by observance of rules that govern the behaviour of hostesses, by friends and the interchangeability of their needs, their willingness to take time, sometimes whole days, in acts of kindness. Marj's friends in British Columbia, too, live gracefully and appear to have the time to show Kate their islands, to listen to her Australian saga. Hasn't Kate had every reason to suppose that Marj's welcome to her in Quebec would be as warm as her friends'?

Marj is in her studio contemplating the red tree, a herald of autumn. She hears the whine of a chain saw, busy at its work of destruction; she sees a brown treeless patch growing. The densely forested mountainside is being clearcut; the voices of thrushes and warblers, the high screech of hawks, have been stilled. Perhaps, she thinks, Kate too is looking dejectedly at the empty landscape—which, splendid as it is on a cloudless day like this one, can refuse to yield an atom of comfort. Marj is fighting with the sickness in her heart, her stony unforgiving. Her time being with Kate has become time choked with dust, with monstrously inflated trivialities. Before Kate's visit Marj almost burst with the joy of minute things, and with her anticipation of Kate's visit to this very place where love has room to revive and flourish. Now Kate is here, with the dangerous look in her pale eyes of a wild creature, caged in the huge dimensions of the view from her window. Both of them are caged, acting fatally each on each. Kate's perception of Marj as inept, thoughtless and unloving has planted itself in Marj like a deadly virus. Kate's remark, "I'm worried about you, Marj," still sounds in Marj's head.

When Marj returns to the house, she finds a torn scrap of paper on the kitchen table, with a note in Kate's handwriting: "I'm not going shopping with you tomorrow," it says. "I'm not cooking Sat. night's dinner—cancel it or cope with it. I'll fit in with whatever you decide—re this and from now until Tuesday. I'd be grateful if you'd post my letter. Thanks."

An ultimatum. Kate's refusals have astonishing power, like the vise of her hand grasping Marj's wrist. You will not get up again, I will not cook, I will not shop. She has fallen into the familiar trap of doing things for people because they are not up to her high standards.

In Quebec their schedule seems as haphazard as the roll of dice. Most of this can be ascribed to Marj's character, but allowances should be made too for the operation of the "Canadian syndrome"—difficult to define but it has, as Kate tries to explain, something to do with not liking to be pinned down. It means leaving space to change your mind. In Quebec Kate is surprised to see labels on Rock Cornish hens saying "May contain giblets." In Australia they either do or don't contain giblets; in Quebec they are as likely to contain giblets as a scratch card is likely to contain a new car. In Quebec, Kate is shocked when Daisy, an old friend, instead of joyfully greeting Kate when she answers Kate's call, says, "Hang on a minute, Charles, I'll call you back." Does this mean that Kate is supposed to restrict her conversation to the minute when Charles is hanging on? In Australia you do not squeeze friends you haven't seen for years into minutes. In Canada, Kate implies, there is a certain carelessness about priorities. Who is Charles, anyway? Technology has pitted two strangers against each other: Kate, who hasn't seen Daisy for ten years and wants to talk, and Charles, waiting in silence for an unknown person (for Daisy does not say, "It's my old friend Kate whom I haven't seen for ten years") to stop talking. And there's the question: is Daisy's "Hang on a minute, Charles, I'll call you back" a not-so-subtle hint to Kate to make it short? Hang on a minute! As if to say, be patient. Kate seems genuinely puzzled. "I've never heard of such a thing!" she says. Marj laughs, for the first time in days. Kate has come back from a two-day visit to Daisy and Jessica, friends from theatre days, and Marj has met her at the bus station. Kate has braved the terrors of Montreal, the French language and bus schedules, and has sailed through them all. She has dropped her stranger's mask and appears to say, "It's you!" And Marj, looking at Kate's glad face, thinks, "It's you!" They hug each other warmly, like good friends, with a friendly meeting of their bodies. "How was it?" asks Marj on the way home. Kate hesitates. "It was all right," she says, implying a reservation? Something about the Canadian syndrome, a theatre person who was supposed to come to tea to meet Kate and forgot, the vagueness of the friends about this breach of manners.

They go back to Montreal, to find stifling heat still trapped in the house. The cracked Quimper mug is still in the bathroom to remind Marj of Brittany, to remind Kate of Marj's inattentiveness to her needs. But Marj has planned some outings—to museums, to the Biodome, and visits with friends. She plans their visit with Anne, her old friend from the film, who lives in a retirement home across the river. A writer-friend calls her; she would like to come, too; she hasn't seen Anne for a long time and has no way of getting there. Hesitatingly, Marj tells Kate. "Virginia doesn't have a car," she says, "and she's a wonderful writer you'll like." Kate explodes. "I'm not going to see Anne," she says. Marj has started to open the front door, they are having dinner down the street. Kate puts her hand on the doorknob. "I won't let you leave the house," she says, "until I've made you understand why I

136

won't go to see Anne." "Go ahead," says Marj. The telephone rings; it is Virginia to say that she can't come with them after all. Kate shows no interest in this intervention by fate. She doesn't want to see Anne anymore, she tells Marj, Marj has spoiled the idea for her.

They go to see the Pellan show, wall after wall of paintings that command joy. Marj in memory is back in Sydney at the Art Gallery; she and Jacky and Kate are looking at the ruthlessly honest paintings of Lucian Freud. Bodies, faces, breasts, genitals speak soberly of how it is. "That's the way it is," Marj sometimes said to Kate when they were talking at mealtime. Kate disliked this phrase. "Nothing is the way it is," she said. "It can always be better." "Or worse," said Marj. Kate saw the glass as half-full, Marj as half-empty; this difference was already forcing them apart. Jacky and Kate did not like the stark realism of Lucian Freud, but to Marj it was a revelation. It made her feel happy. When they drive to the Biodome, Marj parks too far away and they walk an endless way to the entrance. The Biodome, which has been ingeniously designed to fit in the space of the old Velodrome, contains animals and birds in different habitats from Antarctica to the Canadian Shield. They had entranced Marj when she first saw them, but now seem collectively miserable. The capybaras, huge rodents from Argentina, are standing forlornly, muddy and unkempt, at the edge of their pond. The gannets have lost the yellow plumage on their necks, the penguins are moulting, and stand, their backs turned, facing a wall of artificial ice. Marj feels her heart constrict with sadness for the animals in exile, their lives sacrificed so that people can stare at them. She is aware of the irony of the huge concrete columns painted to look exactly like jungle trees, neatly severed at the roof of the cage. How differently Marj felt a year ago with Janet at the Biodome, when she felt the gladness that was part of their uncomplicated friendship. Marj remembers the two hyacinth macaws, vessels of the purest cobalt blue, perched side by side, the scarlet ibises on the edge of their nest full of babies, the burnished golden coats of the little lion tamarins, with serious wrinkled faces and long whiskers, like Chinese sages'.

Today, Marj thinks, the Biodome is the way it is, a painful reminder of decline. Why wouldn't the animals look depressed? They are thousands of miles from home and will never go back. Kate is in a neutral state; Marj cannot read her anymore. Perhaps she has determined not to be read. Perhaps her mind is busy with the work of fashioning a Marj to fit the charges that Kate is accumulating against her; it must be a watertight case, Marj herself must acknowledge its plausibility. Strangely, when a charge is made, Marj feels her identity changing, like Wittgenstein's rabbit-duck, the image that can be either rabbit or duck, depending on how you look at it. Back in the tropical heat of Marj's house, Kate asks out of the blue, "What have you ever done for me from your heart?" Marj thinks hard. "I went to Australia," she says. Australia, a vast continent twenty-three flying hours away; she made this leap of faith for Kate. "I mean *really* from your heart," says Kate. Is this Kate's first move in a logic-session, as when she posed the question, "Why did it take you seven months to answer my first letter?" They haven't had a logic-session since Kate came to Canada. Should Marj say that she wrote her letters *really* from her heart? She has an instant vision of Kate's reply. "You liked the sound of your own voice." True, but love gave wings to my own voice, Marj thinks. At that time Marj and Kate did everything really from their hearts. Now Marj can't remember how "everything" felt. *"Well?"* Marj is silent; no, she can't think of anything, anything untainted by ego—the hope of the kind of pleased response that love finds so easy to make.

Kate and Marj, alone together, are in an unlivable habitat. In the Biodome the animals have lost the lustre of their fur, the radiance of their feathers which can only come from a state of well-being, of being at home. Kate is not at home in Canada; her bright colours fade, her face is haggard. She is bored, like a captive animal. Sometimes the words she utters sound perversely playful. She might be saying, let's see if I can get a rise out of you. Marj, who bubbled with laughter in Australia, does not laugh in Canada; her speech, when she is alone with Kate, reflects the constipation of her mind. Kate tries a little joke. They are driving to lunch with Louise and Marianne. They come to an underpass, the correct way which Marj had unaccountably avoided the day before, only to find herself in a labyrinth of one-way streets. Kate says, "Are you going down under?" "Yes, I am," Marj says, fighting a rising tide of irritation. Yesterday she had lost herself on her own terrain, on a way she had taken dozens of times. Now Kate is reminding her—pleasantly, however. She turns to Marj. "That was my little joke," she says. "Why can't you bloody well laugh at my little joke?" Marj says, "Please, *please*, let's not quarrel on the way to Louise's about why I don't laugh." The two of them have exactly three minutes to transform themselves into apparently loving friends before they greet Louise in her house where harmony reigns. Louise will know by intuition what their climate is, she will hypnotize them by the exercise of her enveloping calm. In her presence it will be easy to laugh. She embraces Kate warmly; her cats seem to recognize a cat-worshipper. Louise has filled the old high-ceilinged house with her own serenity; her ferns and spider plants, which have needed a whole room to grow into huge, unearthly beings, like the plants that grew in northern latitudes before the Ice Age. Marj takes note of the small paintings and drawings she has given to Louise, which have been touched by Louise's magic wand, and have

139

picked up her light. "I like them!" she says with surprise. At lunch the laughter that bubbles out of every meeting of Quebecers punctuates the excited dialogue in French between Louise and Marianne, while Kate looks eagerly from one to the other as though the musical sounds they are making have meaning for her. She looks genuinely happy.

But Louise's gift of grace cannot survive the return to Marj's house, where Kate is suffering time; she does not read, write, listen to music; she does not sit at the table which Marj invitingly cleared for her in her workroom. It is as though the smallest gesture of assent will score a point for Marj in the turgid struggle between them. Yesterday, when the visit to Anne fell through, Marj said to Kate, "I'm under a curse." Kate looked hard at her; she said without raising her voice, "You know *why*, don't you?" "I suppose so," said Marj dully. Each was tied to the behaviour of the other, circling around and around, cause and effect, like a dog chasing its tail.

Kate and Marj leave distances between each other, they do not hold hands or kiss each other goodnight. Marj thinks, I should break this stalemate; it's intolerable. Early one morning, she goes into Kate's room. Kate is lying on her back, staring at the ceiling; her expression does not change. Marj eases herself into the big bed and Kate turns on her side. Their bodies touch matter-of-factly, without magnetism, like two cats, with neither displeasure nor nostalgia, with neutral ease. Marj takes Kate's warm hand, there is not the faintest answering pressure. They do not say a word. Then Marj says, "I guess I'd better go and do something about breakfast." Kate turns abruptly toward the wall and pulls the bedclothes over her head. Why has she made her absurd gesture, Marj thinks, which has proved nothing except that neither can move a fraction of an inch toward the other? Each is afraid; of what—of being violently rejected or of yielding? "The awful daring of a moment's surrender." Eliot knew about the tensions, as strong as steel cables, that keep lovers apart.

Later in the day, Kate makes one of her Delphic pronouncements. "You're ready to jump into bed with me anytime, but I'm not like that," she says. In her head she has fashioned a new image of Marj, "like that," one she needs for her Case. It is her first potshot at the delicate structure they had spun out of trust and intuition in the time when they knew that they loved each other, long before they met. It held fast when they met with a shock of recognition at the Sydney airport, and embraced each other with wordless passion in Kate's apartment. Neither thought, I'm not "that way," they were a way that Marj, at least, was sure they shared.

Alone with Marj in Marj's house, Kate says, "I love you but I don't like you." In Canada Kate knows that dislike can go hand in hand with love. Shakespeare might agree, Marj thinks, remembering how Beatrice and Benedick seem to detest each other. But the audience knows that they are really in love and is waiting breathlessly for them to come out with it.

Marj would like to tell Kate that she doesn't like her either. She doesn't agree that love doesn't alter when it alteration finds. Shakespeare must have said this before his love had been severely tested, when he was in the first being-in-love state which will go on forever. "My love and lover, with whom I'm mated for life," Marj wrote to Kate before Kate came to Canada. Since she arrived, they have looked at each other once with friendliness, they have embraced then with real affection—when Kate came back from her visit to her friends. Didn't it seem in that instant that each had a deep feeling of relief?

On the day of Marj's birthday party for Kate, they are strangers and Kate has her cool questioning look. Each shuts herself into her room and dons her party clothes. Kate is wearing her black outfit and scarlet tie, Marj a pale linen shirt and black pants. They have put on their glad faces, for guests begin to pour in and soon there is a swelling clamour of voices. Marj is in her own whirlpool; she catches sight of Kate sitting on the stairs. She has made friends, is engaged in earnest conversation, she is in one of her elements, party air, which she breathes deeply and easily, though her face, Marj notes, looks strained. When the birthday cake for Kate appears, they are both called upon to make speeches, and they stand with their arms around each other's shoulders. Surely in each head there must be the same impulse to say, "Look, dear friends, why pretend? We are not lovers, we are barely friends. In the space of almost seven weeks we have shown affection for each other once." But their friends have been cheered by delicious catered finger-food and a big bowl of kir on the dining room table and have welcomed the bottles of malt whisky that Marj had the sense to provide. Kate and Marj will pretend for them and for themselves, too, and they say something appropriate— that they have crossed an ocean and a continent to meet each other, that it was a meeting foreseen by the planets. Marj does not know what she is saying; she hears applause and laughter for them both from her dear friends who wish them well and who love the idea of love.

When the last guests have left, Kate says, "It was a great party. You must be tired, darling. You go to bed and I'll clear up, it won't take a minute." Marj thanks her and starts up the stairs, her feet dragging. Kate is standing at the foot of the stairs; she begins to talk, like Scheherazade, spellbinding talk meant to arrest Marj's determined disappearance. Marj takes another step up, with the certainty that once again, she is infuriating Kate.

"Your friends laughed at my jokes," says Kate suddenly, "but you're bored out of your silly mind!" "But you told me to go to bed," says Marj. "Then go to bed!" Marj will go to bed, just as she always goes to bed. A prudent voice whispers in her to protect herself, and now advises her to get some sleep, even though Kate is visibly desperate to exist, to be listened to, desperate for Marj to choose her rather than her own well-being. Has Marj ever stayed up till dawn listening to a needy friend? No, she has a horror of losing the time of the next day, whatever joy it may contain, of its fizzling away, the way days do after a sleepless night. "I'll be nice tomorrow, I'll be thoughtful, I'll make up for going to bed now, if only...." Marj thinks. Kate's angry voice is following her upstairs.

The next day contains no joy. The two days before Kate leaves for Australia are neutral and lifeless; neither moves toward the other. They are both exhausted, either by feeling or by not-feeling. They take a taxi to the airport and stand facing each other before Kate goes through security. They embrace with an exhausted surge of friendly warmth, the shackles fall off and each is her good self again. They wave to each other just before Kate disappears. Marj, on her way back to Montreal, luxuriates in the back seat of the taxi, in the warm summer air that blows in on her and brings her back to life.

Chapter Ten

Each goes back to her own life, her house full of silence. Marj takes back the pronounced shape of her habits, gets up early, goes to bed early, eats summary meals and stretches leftovers. She resumes work on *The Time Being*, not the time with Kate that has just passed, suffocated and gasping for breath, but their newborn time, the beginning through a chance dialogue between two old women, each imagining the other with growing joy. "Moderato ma appassionato," Marj wrote Kate. Marj relives her memories while she and Kate are deconstructing their failure. Ahead of them lie months of disagreement with no hope of compromise, for even with agreed-upon facts, their conclusions are opposite. They entrust this delicate task to written words. But first Kate must clarify the nature of small tasks she has left to Marj—animal drawings from Australia which must be framed (or left unframed) and distributed correctly to friends. She writes Marj meticulous directions. She wants to give the wombat to Winnie, she says, and the possum to Marj and the roo to Marianne, instead of to Danny. "So I hope you haven't mentioned the kangaroo to Danny," and Kate hoped that Marj hadn't told Winnie that her wombat was not being framed and Marianne that her roo was being framed. She had explained this to Marianne, but Marianne may have forgotten because of the Canadian syndrome, says Kate.

Kate sends Marj a postcard from Oliver, the cat, with a message in Oliver's handwriting, a reminder of the time, pre-Australia, when Oliver's postcards, his dropped "aitches" and dubious grammar, delighted Marj. The postcard shows a photograph of a brushtail possum. What possesses Marj to thank the possum for Oliver's message? Kate writes back, refers to Marj's "thinking Oliver's card had been sent by brushtail; had she (Marj) not bothered to read Oliver's appalling handwriting?!" Once again Marj comes up against the immutable reality of something she has done and cannot undo; it has been formed from the fuzzy stuff of her carelessness—obviously, she had not bothered to read Oliver's appalling handwriting—for here is the evidence, incontrovertible, that Marj had not read Oliver with her old love for and attention to Kate. The real Oliver was one of Kate's cast of imaginary characters, the literate cat who dropped his "aitches." Has Marj left unremembered those things which she ought to have remembered? People do not forgive you your forgetfulness, she thinks.

Now Marj is forgetting the importance of the happiness she lived with Kate; worse, she is remembering, not the overwhelming evidence of the good times they had, the good substance Kate has given her of her life, but the hiccups, only the hiccups. Or "our its," as Kate now calls them, for each has her unnegotiable "it." Kate would like further discussion of these "its" avoided. She describes this avoidance as "a way of referring to our difficulties in a very objective way, allowing our obviously different interpretations." The way of silence.

Words get them nowhere. "I can't seem to grasp what it is that *you* feel about me, about us," Kate wrote soon after she got back to Australia. Marj assembled her memories and analogies, remembered scenes in which she was the object of Kate's anger. She remembered how her comparison of Kate's logic to a Procrustean bed had backfired, how Kate had blown up the metaphor for intolerable pressure to fit the old myth of the tyrant who cut off (or stretched) his guests' legs to fit his bed. This time Marj chose a more plausible, a more familiar metaphor. "My back goes up when you *insist* on an answer not as though you love me but because you are absolutely determined *to have an answer,* i.e. as a parent would be determined *('Answer me!')* or a headmistress." Kate found this image "wonderfully unpleasant." She made it clear to Marj that if she could think of her *"in these terms, even for a moment"* it implied that Marj's head was "full of 'congealed matter' (thought-stones!) that has been there since childhood, that is absolutely crackproof!" "Thought-stones," the title of Marj's article about people's defensive reactions to perceived threats, their automatic responses like stones hurled from a catapult, had inspired a paper by Kate: "A Response to Marj's Mind-Changing." Lucid and rational, it is about the ideal uses of rationality, the climate in which rational arguments must take place, namely, a meeting between people whose minds are already open. Marj's paper is about what inhibits rational argument, the intervention in discussions between human beings of the shadow-person who does not want to be wrong. The shadow-Kate has in her the actor-priest who has given her his perfect command over his voice, an orchestra of sounds, from the triumphant shout of brasses to the birdsong of a solitary flute. She is also the twin-face she sees in the mirror, who says, "You are like me, unable to say no, and like your father, too, sick of being good, of people's expectations, turning on them and on yourself. We will continue our quarrels in you and tear you apart."

Kate, however, suggests in her response to Marj's "Thought-Stones" that open minds have been purified, like filtered water, they have been trained always to be open and to thrive on difficulty and doubt. They cannot be polluted, as Marj believes, by the clamour of voices in their genes, anger with as many lives as a cat, ageless emotions, self-generating, an infallible memory for injuries to the self.

They are incompatible in most ways, Kate writes. They have different expectations and hopes, different ideas of commitment, different perceptions each of the other. Kate can only feel free to tell her life story in public from the safety of a committed relationship; Marj can only feel free without commitment. Each has an "it" that does not permit compromise. Kate's "it" is "my need for your understanding and acceptance of my 'logic.'" Marj's "it" is her non-acceptance of *Kate's* logic. She boils it down to two angry words: ANSWER ME! Kate replies that of course she insisted. "YES," she writes, "The outcome was more knowledge of you, more nourishment for my infant love." Kate will say that she was not angry, that in her natural anxiety to know Marj's values she "raised her voice." She has already said that she is completely non-violent, that she can hardly find it in herself to kill a fly. Marj has a vivid memory of Kate's stricken face in her dining room, when Marj pursued a giant cockroach around the wall, cornered it behind a watercolour of roses, and when it emerged, dispatched it with one of Kate's little moccasins.

But if Kate *was* angry, she will argue, post-Canada, it was because Marj with her "sniping" drove her mad with frustration. Back in Australia she will write to Marj that at the Sechelt Festival she was "in the company of Marj, guru and self-centred artist. The provocation was intolerable," she will say. "You got me into a frenzy."

Underneath them, in the calm waters of the time to come, swims Marj's book, a friendly shark, non-threatening, Marj made herself believe before she and Kate met, and in the halcyon time when Kate made a pet out of it and threw it tidbits. Before Marj went to Australia she wrote to Kate, "Sandra thinks our book is a splendid idea; she correctly thought that you may have reservations but I was rather airy about these, not in the sense of knocking them down but in the sense of making them non-lethal to you." They would write the book together, each with her own story, *Truth* and *Real*. That would make it non-lethal. Now, post-Canada, Marj sends Kate the first chapter of *The Time Being*.

Kate writes a long reasoned reply: a letter, along with her own account—*Kate's Time Being*—of their story. She encloses a clipping from a Sydney newspaper, headed "Name the Dull Self in Autofiction." She has been talking to Marj in her mind, she says: "Stop trying to write a novel about love—write an autobiographical piece (as possible material for Marj she recalls the saga of her first letter)...if you leave out the love affair, there's a wonderful story of a growing FRIENDSHIP, through letters and phone calls— potentially a much better 'read' than the heaviness of a love affair being conducted across a vast distance...it could all tell a wonderful story of a new friendship between elderly women, much more universally appealing," she says, than a love story between them. "I was appalled," Kate writes, "to think that Marj herself couldn't see that she was making a huge literary blunder, leaving herself wide open to the severest criticism from all except the lesbian community, who (if it were published) would of course lap up this love story—this latest volume written by and about their heroine and that Australian girl- friend she'd talked so much about." She continues by reminding Marj of "the fact that the affair *didn't* get beyond its romantic beginnings." She writes urgently, with her belief in the power of reason, with the evident belief that Marj will draw back from the brink of the abyss. Her anxious tone, however, suggests that in her view Marj has not understood her right to privacy, nor her right to decide whether Marj should write her book at all. Though

"Kate knew," Kate writes, "that Marj would not do anything to hurt her—the book would only be published if and when Kate was ready.... She simply needed TIME." And anyway, "did she want another person to tell her story, or did she want to tell it herself? She had all kinds of material already written waiting to be developed." But Marj wonders, where is all this time that Kate needs?

In *Kate's Time Being* she reminds Marj of the note Marj attached to Chapter One: "...nothing modest like 'have I written a novel?'...nothing truly honest like 'I know what I'm writing won't protect you'...nothing caring like 'do you mind? is it O.K. by you?' Just a bold statement...'AN INVASION OF YOUR PRIVACY, BUT THAT'S THE SUBSTANCE OF OUR LOVE STORY.'" To Marj it is as truly honest to call her book "an invasion of privacy" and "the substance of our love story" as to pretend that she is sorry or to ask Kate if she minds. To ask Kate if she minds, to sympathize with her plight as subject matter for Marj, would be akin to the heartfelt apology of the Walrus and the Carpenter to the oysters they have happily devoured. Kate perceives Marj's book as deliberate plunder; Marj perceives Kate's rewriting of her book as the cutting out of its heart, its immoderate joy, when she and Kate were more than themselves, when they really *were* in their time being. "For Kate," says Kate, "there was no longer a substantial LOVE story worthy of the telling. She longed for its growth into something more substantial. But the few attempts by Kate (in the Sydney period) to reduce the romanticism with a bit of intellectual or academic toughness, were rejected by Marj, which caused Kate to try to 'pin her down' to an opinion, and in the process to raise her voice. On each occasion, Marj 'won' with an uncharacteristic show of temper that not only shocked Kate, but forced her to give up these attempts."

Marj puzzles over the illogic of Kate's perception of her "uncharacteristic show of temper" as shocking, while her own shows of temper are evidence of her passionate concern for the truth. That's the way it is, Marj thinks; no one likes to be reminded that her unconscious is armed to the teeth. But just as Kate believes that the mind of an enlightened person will remain permanently open, one hundred percent open, so she seems to believe that you can be a Dr. Jekyll without harbouring a Mr. Hyde. On one of her previous trips to Canada Kate's hostess had lent her Marj's autobiography, and her image of Marj before they met was formed by Marj's image of herself and by the nicer-than-life Marj on the screen. "Marj had written," says Kate in *Kate's Time Being,* "about being selfish, puritanical, egocentric, shy and awkward with such apparent insight that Kate had imagined a therapeutic benefit for the author." This benefit, Kate thought, was "the release of a previously repressed generous spirit" and a sensitivity "to the pain and needs of others." But now Kate has realized that these were "erroneous judgements" and that Marj's self-analysis had not changed her for the better. Kate draws up a summary of characteristics of herself and Marj. Marj is puritan, full of certainty, without excesses, egocentric, full of high-class arrogance and high seriousness. Kate is a "sort-of" hedonist, full of doubt, passion, Pollyanna, petit bourgeois modesty, "a sense of life's comedy, especially in relation to oneself."

Kate is emphatic about Marj's inherent puritanism: "She gave the impression of one devoid of excesses of any kind," she says. Marj's sobriety has often been the object of mockery and indignation. "I'd like to tie you down and make you drink," said one host at a cocktail party. But must she make herself sick or stay away from drinkers entirely in order not to make them feel uncomfortable? She likes Dionysians, much as she would like being in the company of a pride of lions as long as they were in a good mood. Kate says, "Marj made no bones about her disapproval of alcohol," but for Marj when she and Kate were alone, alcohol equalled logic—in league with each other, they turned Kate against her. This was not Kate's view: "If, at the table," she says, "there were the slightest hint of a disagreement and of excitability in Kate's voice, Marj would blame the brandies." For Kate, "it was an opportunity for her to TRY to 'pin Marj down' concerning things philosophical, political, social, etc. Kate desperately wanted to know Marj's values, and wanted a bit of substantial debate."

Marj remembers the sensation of being the subject of Kate's desperate searches; she remembers Kate's description of drinkie-times in the past: "the exchange of ideas, the awareness of a mutual savouring of the occasion, a few glasses of wine—not with Marj!—which sometimes intensified the experience." Marj recalls her first vision of Kate, stuck with a person who could neither drink nor dance, and realizes that Kate was also searching for her values, and longing to recreate the mutual savouring of the past. Worst of all, Marj rejected the "academic and intellectual toughness" of Kate's mind. "Is she really an anti-intellectual?" Kate asks in *Kate's Time Being*. For, Kate says, Marj rejects "the whole box and dice of Kate's thinking processes." ("You've turned into a dried-up intellectual!" Marianne threw at Marj in the course of their paradigmatic quarrel.)

Marj has made a drawing of Wittgenstein's rabbit-duck and stares at it fixedly. She finds that by looking into space just beyond it she can see both rabbit and duck at the same time, hold them at the point of the shared eye without either turning into the other.

In *Kate's Time Being* she has, she says, discovered "the Truth," that she and Marj had "always been incompatible in MOST ways." Marj's Chapter One had opened her eyes to the other Marj who had been there all along, the one who got no therapeutic benefit from consideration of her own faults. The one who wrote Kate, when she was surer of their love for each other, that she was this unlikable self, but also the other who loved Kate. "Trust this person," she said, this person who is only trustworthy in the atmosphere of Kate's trust.

Before Marj sent Kate Chapter One, before Kate completed her portrait of the anti-Marj, or, in a return of the old Kate, had vainly tried to make peace; before any fires ravaged the magnificent bush around Sydney and killed thousands of wild animals, before the fires crept into Sydney's suburbs and were turned back, when Kate and her friends watched the bridge turn a dull pink-grey under the sky full of smoke and ashes, Marj sat remembering her New Year's Eve hand in hand with Kate, watching the fireworks from Kate's balcony. In the grand finale the bridge disappeared in the light that sprouted from it, in pink-tinted smoke and a golden rain of harmless fire.

Three months after Kate's trip to Canada, before Marj has sent her Chapter One, it is Marj's New Year's Eve in Montreal and Kate's New Year's Day, a bright warm day in Sydney. Marj telephones Kate, takes instant note of her sweetness and merry laugh and a swimming-up in her consciousness of the first Kate, the irresistible one. "I'm going to spend the new year taking stock of myself," Kate says. Last night, she says, she sat alone on her balcony watching the most spectacular fireworks ever over the bridge. She sat watching, she says, holding a last drinkie in her hand and thinking about her resolutions for the new year. "I've made a resolution, not to do everything my friends want me to do." She gives a list of reasons for not having invited a friend to watch the fireworks with her, the reasons she has given to herself—"I was tired," etc. She had heard her Pollyanna voice saying, "Sheila will feel lonely on New Year's Eve. Why not invite her to watch the fireworks with you? Company for you, too," Pollyanna implied. Kate was proud of her decision, as momentous as the refusal of a cigarette when you have vowed to give up smoking, and are tempted as fiercely as ever. She will give up being good, she will work on *Frances*, her autobiographical novel.

Kate: I feel your presence here.

Marj: I feel my presence there…is the jacaranda in bloom?

Kate: The streets are carpeted with purple flowers.

Marj: Is the frangipani blooming?

Kate: Yes, it's in full bloom and I pick up the blossoms under the tree (do you remember the tree up the street?) and put them in bowls. I connect you with the frangipani…. I don't know why I thought about you today, sitting at my little desk, wearing my three-quarter length pants and my short-sleeved shirt. You were looking up at me. Do you remember those ribbed blue and white pants you wore and my white piqué shirt?

Marj: Of course I do!

Kate: Are you happy?

Marj: Yes, I suppose I'm happy. Not the way I was happy this time last year. That was a special kind of happiness.

Kate: Yes.

Marj: We're beginning to sound like Noel Coward— "You're looking very lovely in the moonlight, Amanda."

Kate: (laughs her Australian laugh, her musical peal of laughter) I'll never fall in love again.

Marj: Me neither.

Kate: I love you.

Marj: (mumbles) Yes...

I loved the you you were with the me I was, Marj thinks. Before they met, Kate wrote to Marj, "Our worst selves are in love with each other," stating one of love's pet illusions—of the worst self born again, converted by the best self. In the New Year, purified by resolutions, the worst selves have declared an amnesty, have put on their innocent carnival garb of "two elderly women" who still share bright memories of their love. In the New Year they will affirm their incompatibilities, will forgive and unforgive; each will listen to the hum of her self's voices, all those selves in herself, each in her own way endeavouring to "see the truth slant."